MY BEDTIME BOOK OF

Two-Minute
Stories

MY BEDTIME BOOK OF

Two-Minute Stories

EDITED BY ROSEMARY GARLAND

Illustrated by Tony Escott and Sally Wellman

for
Lillian Vernon Corp.
510 South Fulton Ave.
Mount Vernon, NY 10550

GROSSET & DUNLAP · Publishers · NEW YORK

Introduction

"Tell me a bedtime story" is a cry that can bring dismay to even the most well-meaning Mother, especially as it always seems to come when patience is at an end and minutes seem like hours. MY BEDTIME BOOK OF TWO MINUTE STORIES is designed to fill the needs of the child at such a moment, without stretching the adult's good humor to its limits. Here are 58 stories, each of which will take but two minutes to read. The stories are new, appealing, and instructive, in a subtle and entertaining way. The pictures are a delight to the eye and a stimulus to the imagination. With MY BEDTIME BOOK OF TWO MINUTE STORIES in hand, you can afford to spoil your children. Don't just read them one story, read them two!

List of Stories

The Story of Jeremy and Lollipop Brown

Jeremy woke up one morning and heard a very funny noise. It sounded like somebody blowing his nose, but what a big blow it was! Jeremy hopped out of bed and looked out of the window—to the park in front of his house. What do you think was there? A great big gray elephant with his trunk up in the air. It was the elephant making the big noise.

Well, what would you have done? Jeremy was so excited he shouted for his Mother and Daddy to come and see. They watched the elephant while his Daddy told Jeremy all about the big circus that was coming to the park that day.

It was lovely for Jeremy. All day he watched the caravans come and the cages with the lions and tigers and all the lovely horses and lots and lots of people. And next day Mother took him to see the circus. Inside the enormous tent were big bright lights although the sun shone outside. First, the band played very loud and in came the ringmaster, a very important man in a red coat and a black top hat.

Then came the clowns and Jeremy loved them all. The tall thin one with great big feet. The little tiny one with bright orange hair and most of all he loved Mr. Brown, the one in the baggy check pants. He was the funniest of them all in his special automobile that kept falling to bits and when it did Mr. Brown laughed and laughed. Jeremy liked the seals who played the trumpet, the prancing horses with pretty ladies riding, the lions and tigers and the man on the high wire. The elephants danced and the Shetland ponies did tricks and everybody had a wonderful time. Then it was time to go home.

Before he went to bed Jeremy told his Daddy all about the circus and said thank you very much to his mother for taking him.

In the morning, the circus was still there so after breakfast, Jeremy sat by his bedroom window and had a lovely view of all the circus people doing their work. They swept out the caravans, hung up the washing and carried buckets of water and everybody was very busy.

Soon Jeremy saw Mr. Brown come out of his caravan, sit on the steps and start to eat his breakfast. He didn't look quite the same without his funny painted face, but Jeremy knew him by his baggy check pants. He was excited and he called out "Hello Mr. Brown" and waved and Mr. Brown waved back and said, "Come and sit on my steps if you like, but watch how you cross the road".

So, down the stairs Jeremy went and Mother took him over the road and said "Good Morning" to Mr. Brown and said they had seen him the day before. Mr. Brown smiled and said he would take Jeremy back at lunch time. So after he had finished his breakfast, Mr. Brown took Jeremy by the hand and they went to see the animals.

It was fun. Mr. Brown knew them all. Rajah and Leo the lions. Tessa and Tonto the tigers and Rosie and Daisy the elephants. And all the animals knew Mr. Brown. There were circus children too and they came running to Mr. Brown shouting "Hello, Lollipop Brown—how are you today?"

That's funny, thought Jeremy and he was just going to ask why, when Mr. Brown reached into the big pocket of the baggy check pants and brought out a handful of lollipops and gave one each to all the children. Jeremy got a yellow one—wasn't that a lovely surprise!

Soon Mr. Brown took Jeremy home because it was time for Mr. Brown to go and paint his funny face on before the circus started again. Off he went with a laugh and a wave, across to his caravan.

Next day, all the caravans had gone when Jeremy woke up, but he will never forget his friend Mr. Lollipop Brown.

Mr Mortimer and His secret

All the children in the park know Mr. Mortimer, the old tortoise with the black top hat. Every day in the summer you can see them talking to him.

Mr. Mortimer is quite old of course, his little head and neck are all wrinkly, but his black eyes are shiny bright and twinkling. He loves the children and they are very kind to him. Every day they bring him carrots, bits of sweet apple and fresh green lettuce leaves which he likes very much. Like all tortoises, Mr. Mortimer goes for a long sleep in the winter, so you can never see him then, but as soon as the warm days come and the sun comes out, back comes Mr. Mortimer just the same as ever.

One hot Thursday, Ben, the man who looks after the park, decided to take some sandwiches for lunch and have a picnic instead of pedalling home on his bicycle at lunch time. Mrs Ben gave him lovely sandwiches, some with banana and honey, and

some with egg. There were far too many for Ben to eat all by himself and he thought he would give some to the tortoise, but Mr. Mortimer wasn't there.

Ben looked everywhere. In the flower beds, by the swings, in the sand pit and all round the paddling pool, but there was no sign of Mr. Mortimer. "Well that's a puzzle," said Ben to himself, "I wonder where he is?" Ben had to get on with his work after lunch of course, but all afternoon he kept looking and even when it was time for him to go home, he still had not found Mr. Mortimer. But next morning when Ben

got to work, there was the tortoise waiting for him just as before.

The next Thursday Mr. Mortimer disappeared again, and the next week and the next. Ben wondered where he went, but it didn't really matter; the park is big and Mr. Mortimer is quite safe inside.

Perhaps Ben would never have found out, if it had not been for the twins. Nearly every day they come to the park with their Mother and she sits and knits while they play in the sand pit, or on the swings. If it is warm enough, they sail boats on the paddling pool. One day the twins had a birthday and one of the birthday presents was a yellow kite with lots of colored ribbons on it. Ben got it up in the wind and then the twins held the string while the kite danced and sailed up in the sky. Then came a big gust of wind and what do you think happened? The twins let go of the string and the kite sailed away. Off in the wind all alone, off over the park, high in the sky.

Well, the twins were miserable because nobody knew how to catch the kite. But along came Ben and he said "Cheer up, twins. I'll pop across the park on my bicycle and if I'm quick I might catch the kite" and off he went pedalling away very fast. He went past the swings, past the sand pit and past the paddling pool, right over to the gardens where the big bird cages are. It is quite a long way, over on the other side of the park. And, that's where he saw the kite, still flying but caught by the string on the little tree by the big parrot's cage.

Very carefully, Ben unwound the string and was just getting ready to pedal back to the twins, when he saw Mr. Mortimer. There he was inside the cage with the parrot. The big old parrot was sitting on his perch, talking and chuckling away to Mr. Mortimer and Mr. Mortimer was on the floor of the cage with his black top hat upside down beside him. The top hat was upside down because it was full of carrots, bits of sweet apple and fresh garden lettuce leaves. Mr. Mortimer and his friend the parrot were having a picnic. What do you think of that?

Ben smiled and said "Fancy that"—but he kept very quiet so they didn't know he was there. Of course, Ben has never told anybody about the secret of Mr. Mortimer who is always missing from the park on Thursdays after lunch.

The Rosebud teapot

Once upon a time there was a little teapot and she had rosebuds dotted about all over her. She was very pretty and she was a real china teapot. Do you know how she knew she was made of real china? If you held her up to the light, you could see the light shining through. And you can't do that with a teapot which is not made of real china.

Rosebud knew she was something special because she was always kept in the best china cupboard and she was only brought out on Sundays and on very special occasions.

But one day someone was very careless and knocked her spout on the kitchen tap, and chipped it. Poor Rosebud! It hurt quite a bit and after that she cried every time she tried to pour out the tea.

"We can't use this teapot for best any more," they said. "because the spout is chipped and dribbles on the table."

Rosebud didn't mind because now she was used every day and she loved being kept busy. They put a sort of sponge collar round her neck to catch her tears, and to stop the tea dripping on to the tablecloth.

But another sad thing happened. This time someone dropped her little rosebud hat and broke it! Poor Rosebud watched them throw her lid into the trash can. Now she felt very shabby because she never went out without a hat in the old days.

"Now we really can't use her any more!" they said. And she was pushed into the back of a dark cupboard. Poor Rosebud was soon covered with dust and no one ever washed her pretty dress any more.

One day after a long time without seeing anyone at all, someone took her out of the cupboard and said: "You can have this for your Jumble sale. It's no good to us any more."

They bundled Rosebud into a box with a lot of other old things and away she went, she didn't know where.

She landed up on a stand in the Town Hall Jumble Sale. She sat sadly surrounded by a lot of other sad things, worn out old things which someone had once loved, but didn't love any more.

Lots of hands moved all over the stall, picking things up and putting them down again. No one bothered about Rosebud until almost the end of the day. A little girl picked her up and said: "It is sweet, isn't it?" Her mother said, "Yes, dear, but its spout is

chipped and it has no lid. But it's real china, you know."

"How do you know?" asked the little girl.

"Hold it up to the light," said her mother.

The little girl held it up to the light and saw the light shining through. "It's only twenty five cents," said the lady at the stand.

"I'll take it," said the little girl.

"Whatever do you want that for?" asked her mother.

"I'll show you when I get home," said the little girl. And she took little Rosebud home very carefully. She loved little Rose-

The Seasons

Spring comes when Winter goes,
Hello flowers, good-by snows.
Summer's warm, the grass is cool,
The frog goes plop! into a pool.
Buzzing bees and Autumn trees,
Here comes Winter. Now we freeze!

bud and little Rosebud was so glad to be wanted again.

"I've never had anything made of real china before," said the little girl.

The little girl went out into the woods, and when she came back she filled little Rosebud with primroses.

"Don't they look lovely?" said her mother. "That was a good little flower vase you bought at the Jumble sale."

The primroses smelt so sweet, and Rosebud felt so clean, and she lived on the little girl's bedside table for always.

Nobby the Proud Horse

Everybody said that Nobby was a fine looking horse. He had a beautiful brown coat which gleamed as though it had just been polished, and was soft to touch, like velvet.

His master, Farmer Jones, was very proud of him. But he made so much fuss of him that Nobby began to think he was better than anyone else. And he stopped speaking to his old friends, Ned, the gray donkey and Floss, the sheep dog.

His friends were upset. "You should remember you are only a cart horse," Ned told him. "You are not a race horse."

Nobby didn't answer. He went on pulling at the grass while he waited for Farmer Jones to come for him.

But Farmer Jones didn't come that day. Or the next day. Or the day after.

Nobby grew worried. What could be the matter?

At last he decided to speak to Ned. Ned didn't know. So he asked Floss when he saw her running across the field.

"Didn't you know?" said Floss. "Farmer Jones has bought a tractor. I don't suppose he'll need you anymore, the tractor can do all the work you used to do."

Not want him anymore? Nobby was upset. He just couldn't believe it. He wandered across the field and squeezed through a gap in the hedge and trotted off down the lane.

He wasn't sure where he was going. Just somewhere where someone would want him.

Suddenly he stopped. What was that noise? Crunch, crunch. Oh, it was a steamroller coming towards him.

He reared up on his hind legs and snorted

with fright. Then he turned and raced back the way he'd come.

At that moment Floss bounded round a bend in the lane. "Stop, Nobby," she barked when she saw him.

Following close behind her was Farmer Jones. "Whoa, there old fellow," he cried. "Steady does it."

At the sound of his voice Nobby slowed down. "What's this all about then, eh?" said Farmer Jones as he came up and patted him. He gave him a sugar lump from his pocket. "That's better then," he said as Nobby licked it up from his hand.

"Now we'll go home, and you can help me pull that stupid new tractor of mine out of the mud," said Farmer Jones, as they all walked along quietly together.

" 'Stupid new tractor?' He said 'stupid new tractor'," thought Nobby to himself. "And he's asking me to help him. So he does want me after all."

He gave a little neigh of delight at the thought of it.

"Feeling better?" asked Farmer Jones as

they heaved the tractor out of the mud.

"Tractors are all right when the weather is fine," he said. "They're a nuisance when the ground is sticky like it is now. That's when we need a good strong horse like you, Nobby. And by the look of the sky we're going to have more rain. So I shall be needing you a lot, old fellow. Your holiday's over."

Holiday? Is that all it was? What a silly horse he'd been.

"Hello Ned, hello Floss," he called out when he saw his friends. He was never too proud to speak to them anymore. He was just grateful to have such good friends.

In a lane full of bends,
Is a house full of friends,
With a pond at the back,
Where the ducks go, Quack!

There I love to roam,
Even though it's far from home,
Near the house in the plain,
Down the end of the lane.

Extra bouncy

Johnny's ball was extra bouncy. It bounced and bounced and bounced right up into the air. It bounced into the trees. It bounced on the roof. It was big and bright and orange. And when it seemed to lose its bounce just a little, Daddy pumped it up again with a bicycle pump. He pumped and pumped and pumped.

"There," said Daddy. "Now it will bounce right over the chimney tops."

"Will it really?" asked Johnny.

And that's what happened. Johnny bounced it hard and away went the big orange ball, right over the chimney tops. It was the biggest bounce of all—but it never came back again. Johnny was very sad about his orange ball. He told Old Toddy, the gardener, all about it.

"Never mind," said Toddy. "If you wake up very, very early one morning and look out of your window, you *might* see your extra bouncy ball again."

Johnny woke up early the next morning. "I didn't see the ball," he said to Toddy.

"You didn't wake up early enough," said Toddy.

So Johnny tried again and again. At last he woke up before it was really and truly light. And there was his big orange ball sitting right on top of the roofs of the houses on the very edge of the world. Toddy was right. Johnny gazed at his ball and watched it as it slowly went up, up, up into the sky. Up, up, up it went. Johnny quickly dressed and ran out into the garden. But when he got there, he couldn't see his big orange ball anywhere. There was only the sun behind the clouds.

"It really must be an extra bouncy ball,"

said Toddy when Johnny told him all about it. "I mean, to go right up into the sky and out of sight—like an airplane."

"Will it ever come down again?" asked Johnny.

"Yes," said Toddy. "But extra high bounces take extra long time to come down again, haven't you noticed that?"

"Yes," said Johnny. "I have."

"Well then, I should think it might take a whole day to bounce down again," said Toddy. "It might come down after you've gone to bed."

So Johnny waited until his mother had said good night. Toddy had said: 'It's no use looking out of your bedroom window. It will come down on the other side of the house.' So Johnny ran to his mother's bedroom and peeped out of the window. There was the big orange ball coming down, down, down slowly until it touched the roofs of the houses on the edge of the world. Then it slowly disappeared.

In the morning he told Toddy that he thought the ball had gone forever. "No," said Toddy." I expect that ball is still bouncing and bouncing."

"You must not stop looking for it because the bounces get smaller and smaller. And soon the ball lies perfectly still."

But Johnny didn't have to wait long. He turned round, and there in the long grass was his bright orange ball. "It can't have been here all the time," he said.

"No," said Toddy. "I know it wasn't there yesterday because I was busy gardening just there."

Do you think it was Johnny's ball which he saw on the edge of the world?

I think it was the sun. On one side of the house it was rising in the early morning, and on the other side of the house it was going down again—just like a big bouncing ball.

What do you think?

Candystripe's Cousin

You can see at once that Candystripe is a very unusual cat. For one thing he always wears a yellow knitted woollen sweater, and for another, although he is snow white all over, he has one and only one, long black whisker. He has plenty of white whiskers of course, all cats have those but that black whisker is very special indeed, and very unusual.

Candystripe is a happy cat. He lives in a warm house, gets plenty of milk to drink and fish to eat and, when he feels like a rest, there's a clean basket with plenty of soft cushions for him to sleep on. Of course, plenty of people live in the house with him. A Mother and a Daddy—sometimes a Granny comes—there are two different Grannies and two Grandpas—and there is also a boy who lives there all the time. When the boy was little, Candystripe used to play with him, but he goes to school now, and when he is at home he always seems to be playing with another boy—called Cousin.

Sometimes, when the boys would play, Candystripe would watch them and wish he had a cousin—because boys don't play cat games and cats can't play boys' games and it must be nice, he thought, to be able to play with somebody else.

One warm day, Candystripe was lying on the garden wall, stretched out in the sun, watching the boys playing with a tent on the lawn. His eyes began to close and he was nearly asleep, when, suddenly the long black whisker twitched.

Candystripe opened one eye and looked at the whisker. It twitched again, twice and then again, just to make sure that Candystripe was awake. He was by then, of course, wide-awake. Down he jumped from the wall, running fast towards the garden gate, over the top and off as fast as his legs would go. Soon he got to the village park and there in the middle—where it always was—was the duck pond. There was just one little water hen swimming on the pond that day, but she was in a terrible state. She swam backwards and forwards fussing.

As soon as she saw Candystripe by the pond, she opened her beak and made such a noise. It was just then that Candystripe saw it—"Oh I see" he said, "that's what she is so bothered about—somebody has lost a fur glove in the pond."

And there it was floating towards him, helped along by the water hen.

Candystripe watched as it came close enough for him to reach out his paw and lift it on to the grass.

He looked at it and then he had another look. Funny sort of glove, he said to himself, it's all fur—and then what do you think happened? *The glove squeaked!* That made Candystripe jump, I can tell you.

"Gloves can't squeak," said Candystripe, but that one did and he listened again. The glove squeaked, twice, and louder this time. So, stretching out his nose, very carefully, Candystripe sniffed the glove. It was little, it was fur and it was soaking wet, but it wasn't a glove, it was a tiny little white kitten.

"What a surprise!" said Candystripe, "what a lovely surprise; you are not an old fur glove at all. What's your name?"

But the little kitten was very shy and she wouldn't say anything.

"We've got to get you dry," said Candystripe. "Come and play in the sun and you'll soon feel fine."

So they played together on the grass and soon the kitten was a dry and happy little bundle of fluff. But she still didn't know her name, and that's when Candystripe said, "Come home with me then, you can live with us and you can be my Cousin. The boy has a Cousin to play with—so you can be my Cousin and we can play together."

And that is what happened. If you ever pass their house, you may see them in the garden, playing cat games. Cousin is growing bigger all the time—but you will always know which one is Candystripe—because he is the one with the long black whisker.

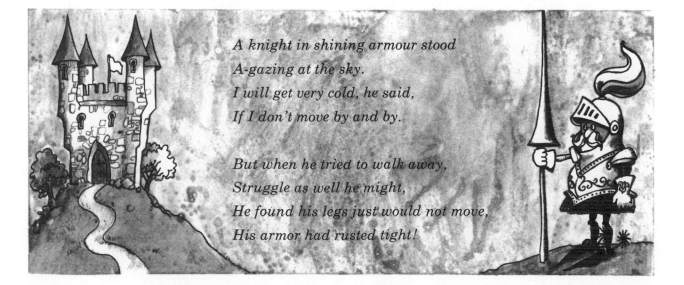

A knight in shining armour stood
A-gazing at the sky.
I will get very cold, he said,
If I don't move by and by.

But when he tried to walk away,
Struggle as well he might,
He found his legs just would not move,
His armor had rusted tight!

The Green Umbrella

The green umbrella was old and shabby. But it had not always been so. Once it had been a beautiful silk umbrella and belonged to a rich lady who lived in a big house.

But she was a careless lady and one day she went for a walk and left the umbrella hanging on some railings in a park.

There it was found by a little man who was a clown, and who worked in a circus.

He took it home to his caravan which he shared with a cat and a dog. Every evening he took the green umbrella into the circus ring where he would ride with it on a very odd-looking cycle.

Sometimes he would perch the green umbrella on the top of his nose. And sometimes on the top of his head. And when he was upside down, as he often seemed to be, the umbrella would be perched on the tip of

his big toe. It never knew where it was going to find itself.

Still, it behaved very well and never once disgraced its master, the clown, by falling down.

Then one sad day it found itself no longer wanted. The clown had some new tricks and the umbrella was thrown onto a rubbish dump.

It wondered what would become of it then. It soon found out.

A tramp picked it up. He seemed very pleased with it and slung it over his shoulder with his lunch tied to its handle, all done up in a red spotted handerchief.

They travelled all over the country together, through towns and villages, past houses and haystacks—they never passed the haystacks at night, they slept in them and very cozy and warm they were.

Then in the morning on they went again, until one day they parted company. They didn't want to part company: it was an accident.

The umbrella fell over into a stream while they were sitting together having lunch. Although the tramp tried to rescue it, the wind blew it away—far away along the stream until it was caught by some rushes and drifted to the bank.

A duck found it. This duck, which was known as a 'Shoveller' duck quickly shovelled some grass and leaves into it and then laid some eggs.

Before long some baby Shovellers were hatched and the umbrella became a nursery for the baby ducks.

But as soon as they were old enough, they all shovelled off and the umbrella was left on its own.

Strangely enough, it didn't mind. It had travelled a lot and seen many things, exciting things too, but now it was tired.

So it settled itself down in the rushes where no one would see it and watched the rest of the world go by.

It saw many Shoveller ducks go by. And it saw summer and winter go by.

When spring came again and fresh flowers bloomed and young birds sang in the trees, the green umbrella felt very much like rising up in the morning breeze and sailing away.

But it didn't. It stayed where it was and gave shelter to all sorts of little animals, who felt safe under the friendly umbrella.

The Greedy Gobbler

Sarah had fifty cents to spend. It was such a lot of money for Sarah that she did not know how to spend it. She went to the little toy shop round the corner and looked at the hundreds of exciting things in the window.

Some of the toys were much more than fifty cents—the sort that Aunts buy for little girls and boys. And some were less than fifty cents—the sort of toys Sarah bought with her weekly pocket money.

Sarah looked and looked. Suddenly she saw something that was *exactly* fifty cents —and she immediately knew that was just what she wanted. It was a yellow glass pig.

She went into the shop and waited to be served. She was very excited and she hoped that no one would buy that funny yellow glass pig before it was her turn.

At last it was Sarah's turn to be served. "Please, I would like to have the yellow pig in the window," she said.

"Ah," said Mrs. Higgins. "I know the one you mean because it is the only one in the shop."

Mrs. Higgins fished about in the shop window. She took a long time because the window was crammed with toys and she didn't want to upset them all. Sarah hopped about from one foot to the other. At last Mrs. Higgins brought it out.

"There," she said. And the funny yellow glass pig winked in the bright light.

"Oh, but it has a slit in its back," said Sarah. "What's that for?"

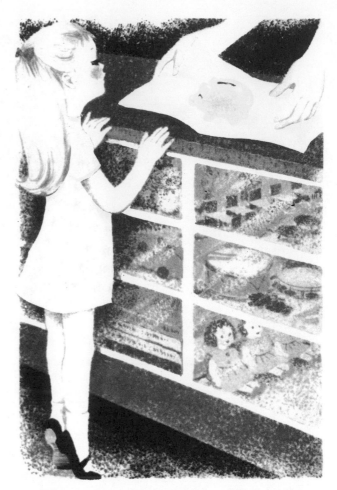

"It's a piggy bank, you know," said Mrs. Higgins. Sarah didn't know what a piggy bank was and she didn't like to ask. "Oh," she said, just a little quietly. She gave Mrs. Higgins the fifty cents and Mrs. Higgins wrapped it up very carefully.

Sarah carried it home very carefully. She didn't even peep in the paper, in case she dropped him.

She showed it to Daddy when she got in.

"Oh, a piggy bank," said Daddy.

And she showed it to Mother and Mother said: "Oh, a dear little piggy bank."

And she showed it to Auntie and Auntie said: "What a sweet little piggy bank!"

And she showed it to Grannie and Grannie said: "What a darling little piggy bank!"

"What *is* a piggy bank?" asked Sarah. Everyone seemed to know except Sarah.

"It's to put your money in," said Grannie.

Sarah looked a little sad; she thought she was going to cry.

"Why, what's the matter?" asked Daddy.

Fisherman's Song

I'd like to catch a BIG fish,
I'd like to catch a few.
But the only thing I ever caught
Was a battered old shoe!

So I throw them dainty morsels,
I throw them lots of bread.
But the only thing I ever caught,
Was a cold in the head!

"Well, first I had some money and no piggy bank," said Sarah. "Now I have a piggy bank and no money!"

Everyone laughed. "Let me be the first to put a penny in," they all said at once. And Daddy and Mother and Auntie and Grannie all put a penny in. That was four pennies, wasn't it? And the little pig gobbled them up and they tinkled inside his tummy.

"I shall call him Gobbler," said Sarah.

"I'll put a penny in every time you bring the newspaper," said Daddy.

"I'll put a penny in every time you go to bed at the right time," said Mother.

"I'll put a penny in every time you take my dog for a walk," said Auntie.

"And I'll put a penny in every time you find my glasses for me," said Grannie.

Sarah brought the newspaper and went to bed at the right time and took the dog for a walk and found Grannie's glasses and everyone popped in their pennies.

"His stomach is getting very full," laughed Sarah. "He *is* a greedy Gobbler!"

The Storks of Strasbourg

Strasbourg is a beautiful old town in France. One day there was great excitement in the streets of Strasbourg. Everyone was staring up at the sky. The storks had arrived.

The first pair were perched on the roof of one of the oldest houses in the town.

Every spring they arrived from the south —from Africa and Egypt. Across the blue Mediterranean sea they flew, to nest in the chimneys of the old Strasbourg houses.

The people were so pleased to see them because they believed the storks were lucky birds.

"While the storks nest in our chimney tops we shall enjoy good fortune," they told one another.

In they flew, these big white birds with black wings, their necks stretched straight out as they wheeled above the houses with their red legs trailing behind them.

Down they came on to the rooftops to find a chimney in which to build a nest. Some of them returned to their last year's nests. Some were unlucky because the winter snows had torn their nests apart and washed them down the steeply sloping roofs.

But some nests needed only a bit of repairing to make them ready for use again.

And so the storks began to be very busy with the work they'd flown so far to do.

And the people of Strasbourg could not stand all day either and watch the storks. They had to be busy too and wait patiently for the exciting day when the baby storks would be hatched.

The birds worked hard. Mr. Stork did most of the hunting for the materials for the nest. He collected lumps of earth, bits of twigs, grass, sticks and paper from wherever he could find them. Mrs. Stork made them into a sort of platform on the chimney top until she had built her large nest.

When at last the nests were all finished, the birds laid their eggs. Some laid three eggs, some four and some five in their nests.

The storks took turns to sit on their eggs. Mr. Stork usually sat on them at night, and Mrs. Stork sat on them during the day.

About four weeks later the eggs hatched.

What a noise and bustle there was up in the chimney tops!

And what appetites those baby storks had! They ate and ate and ate. The parents had to work really hard to fill their tummies.

And so spring passed, and the warm summer, and the young storks grew big and strong and were able to fly around like their parents.

Then one day in autumn the people of Strasbourg looked up and saw that the storks were preparing to leave. The days were getting cold and the storks wanted to fly back to the south, to the warmer lands.

Up in the air they flew, and for a time they seemed to hang there, hardly moving.

Then suddenly there was a great flapping of wings and they were away.

Higher and higher they rose, round and round they circled until at last they disappeared into the blue of the sky.

"Good-by," waved the people in the streets. "Good-by storks. Come back to us in the spring."

They didn't feel sad. Because they knew the storks would return in the spring—as they always did every year.

Waiting for the Dentist

Christopher was waiting for the dentist. He had been there before and he knew that the dentist had a big chair that went up and up when the dentist pumped it with his foot. That was fun. Then the dentist asked him to open his mouth while he poked around inside to see if Christopher's teeth were nice and strong.

Christopher didn't mind very much, but he wished the dentist didn't make him keep his mouth open so long and so very wide!

Christopher and his mother waited in the big room all by themselves at first. Suddenly Christopher saw a big fish tank full of fish.

"Look, mother, that wasn't here last time," he said. And he ran over and watched the fish lazily drifting about amongst the little weeds. One opened and shut his mouth all the time.

"He looks as if *he's* at the dentist!" laughed Christopher. "But he hasn't any teeth, has he?"

"No," said Mother. And they watched the fish for a long time.

Just then another little boy came into the waiting room with his mother, and he was crying. "I don't like the dentist," he kept crying.

But Christopher was still watching the

The Little Bird

This is the tale of the little bird
Who was never seen
And never heard.

Then one fine day he sat upon
The garden barrow
And sang a song!

26

fish. Suddenly he saw the sand heaving about at the bottom of the tank. "Why, there's one trying to bury itself in the sand!" he shouted with excitement.

The other little boy ran across to see.

"Look at this silly fish," said Christopher. "He's nearly disappeared under the sand". Christopher and James, the other little boy, had such fun together chattering about the fish that James forgot to cry any more.

"Look, there's a black one," said James. "He's just popped out from behind that big shell."

"That's called a Black Moll," said his mother.

"Could I have a fish tank at home?" asked Christopher.

"Yes, that would be fun. We will save up and buy a new fish each week," said Mother.

"Can I have a fish?" asked James.

"Yes," said his mother. "We will save up too. We might even win one at a fair. I did when I was a little girl. I took it home in a plastic bag full of water!"

Christopher and James talked and talked about which kind of fish they would buy first. They chattered so much that James didn't mind when the dentist's nurse came in and called him. He waved good-by to Christopher and off he went.

"He didn't have to wait long, did he?" said Christopher.

"Well I'm glad the time went so quickly," said Mother. "It was watching the fish that made the time pass. And it made you both forget all about the dentist."

May Tree Blossom

All the animals on May Tree Farm seemed to be having babies. Mrs. Grunt the pig was the first with her ten piglets.

"Aren't they wonderful?" she grunted through the gate of her sty as Mrs. Hen passed by.

Mrs. Hen peeped through at the piglets who were rolling and squealing in the straw. "Cluck," she cried. "I like their curly tails."

Mrs. Hen hadn't any babies. But she had been thinking that she would like some for a long time. She sat on her nest most of the day and wouldn't come off it when Mrs. Farmer collected the eggs twice a day.

"She ruffles her feathers and tries to peck me," Mrs. Farmer told her husband.

"Well, we'd better let her hatch out some chicks," he said. "There's an empty chicken house over in the Long Field. It just needs cleaning out a bit."

So Mrs. Farmer and young Billy and little Sue cleaned out the chicken house and put fresh straw in the nest box.

Then Mrs. Farmer took ten eggs from her basket and laid them carefully in the nest.

When Mrs. Hen saw them she clucked with delight. She hurried into the nest box and there she stayed, only coming out for food and exercise each day. Soon she had hatched out ten pretty baby chicks.

"Tell Mrs. Grunt I have ten babies now," she called to Dilly Duck who was passing by with her ducklings on the way to the pond.

Dilly Duck promised to tell Mrs. Grunt.

She also told Nanny Goat as she passed through her field. Nanny Goat had just had twin kids and had only come back into her field that morning.

"We've been shut up in the goat shed for ages," she said. "My kids were getting rather naughty shut up in there. They're better now that they can peep through the hedge and see the lambs."

"Quack," said Dilly. "I didn't know Mrs Baa had any lambs."

She peeped through the hedge. "Why," she said. "All the sheep have lambs. There are dozens of them skipping about all over the field."

"Quack, follow me carefully," she called to her ducklings as they waddled through a

hole in the hedge behind her. "I don't want you getting lost among all these lambs."

Some of the lambs ran to hide behind their mothers as Dilly and her ducklings passed by.

"Quack," Dilly said to them. "We won't hurt you, we're just on our way to the pond, that's all."

Over by the pond stood Kitty, the brown mare. She was licking her new born foal who was lying on the grass.

"Farmer will be surprised," she told Dilly.

Farmer *was* surprised when he came across the field and saw the foal. Already she was up and standing firmly on her four little legs.

"Come Billy, come Sue," he called as they came out of the cowshed. "See what we have here."

"Oh," cried Sue. "She is the nicest of all the new babies. What shall we call her?"

"Let's call her 'Blossom'," said Billy. "Because she was born when the May blossom's out."

Everybody on the farm loved Blossom. She was the favorite. Bella the cow had a fine young calf called Brownie but Blossom was the pet of Farmer, Mrs. Farmer, Billy and Sue.

There was a young man
Who wore colored clothes
And had a black mask
And danced on his toes!

He loved a young lady
Whose dress was so fine.
His name was Harlequin
And hers Columbine.

Beaver Lodge

It was winter time and Mrs. Beaver and her children were warm and snug in the living room of Beaver Lodge.

"Tell us how you built our house," said young Bertie Beaver.

"But I've told you *that* story many times," answered his mother.

"Well, I've never heard it," said the littlest beaver of the family.

"Very well," said Mrs. Beaver. "One day, a long time ago, I met your father swimming in this stream. We decided to stay here and to build a house."

"We beavers nearly always build our houses in the middle of a pond, don't we?" said Bertie.

"That's right, dear, it makes us feel safer to live surrounded by water, though some of our relations have their homes in river banks. Anyway, as there wasn't a pond here, we made one!"

"How did you do that?" asked the youngest beaver.

"We built a high wall, called a dam, across the stream to stop the water running away, and as it couldn't run away, it overflowed the banks of the stream and made a pond!"

"What was the dam made of, mother?"

"Trees and branches and stones and mud. We cut down young trees with those sharp teeth of ours, and laid them across the stream; then we stuck them together with mud, and you've seen for yourselves how high the dam is!"

"And then you built Beaver Lodge!"

"Yes, we made an island of sticks and mud and dug out this room in the center of it. To make quite sure that no one sees us coming or going Daddy put the front and back doors below the level of the water."

"It's a good thing we are all such good swimmers, isn't it" said one of the children. "Go on with the story, mom!"

"Well, one day . . ." Mrs. Beaver got no further. There was a loud rustling outside the room and in burst Mr. Beaver.

"The dam has broken!" he cried. "There is no time to lose, we must all help repair it

set about cutting down a tree. Soon, they had bitten through the bottom of the trunks and the little trees splashed into the water. Bertie was waiting and swam off, pushing the trees in front of him.

The other beaver children had scooped up as much mud as they could in their front paws and were also swimming towards the dam.

Very cleverly, Mr. Beaver laid the newly cut trees across the hole in the dam.

"Now, children, drop your mud over the branches—that will keep them in position."

The youngest beaver was the last to bring his mud.

"You've done very well, dear," said his mother.

"Yes, our pond is safe now," said Mr. Beaver, "let's go back and have supper."

As the moon rose over the pond, no one saw the beaver family swim up to their front door. Though Owl, sitting in the willow tree, *thought* he saw the water ripple.

or there will be no water left in our pond!"

The children chattered with excitement.

"Quiet, everyone,' commanded Mr. Beaver. "Now, if you all do exactly as you are told, we shall soon have it mended. There are some young trees on the edge of the river bank. Your mother and I will cut two of them down. Bertie, you will be ready to help push them through the water to the hole in the dam. The rest of you will carry as much mud as you can. We will all meet there."

One by one, the family left Beaver Lodge, entered the water and started to work. They used their webbed back feet and broad, flat tails to help them to swim strongly.

Mr. and Mrs. Beaver reached the bank and climbed out of the water. Quickly, each

The Gold Star

It was Monday morning at the Nursery School.

Roger walked silently along. This was his first day at school and though he felt proud of his book bag hanging from his shoulder, he was not at all sure that he wanted to stay for a whole morning.

At that moment, Roger's friend Christopher, followed by his mother, sped through the gate on his tricycle.

"Hello," called Christopher.

"Hi, Chris," answered the new boy.

"Don't worry," said Christopher, "we have lots of fun, you'll like it, Come on!"

Roger hesitated, looked up at his mother and swallowed a funny lump in his throat.

"Good-by, Mom," he whispered.

She smiled. "I'll be here for you at noontime, waiting to hear all about it."

Mrs. Fisher, who was in charge of the Nursery School, was standing at the door.

"Hello, Roger," she said kindly, "I *am* glad you are joining us. Come along in, dear. Put your overall on, because we shall be painting later this morning."

Roger hung up his coat and Christopher, in a bright green overall, waited for him while he struggled into his scarlet smock.

Together the two friends walked into a room filled with boys and girls making a great deal of noise. There were small-size tables and chairs and a large Notice Board.

"Our paintings are pinned up on that board," explained Christopher "and every morning the best one has a gold star stuck on it."

"Oh," said Roger.

Mrs. Fisher clapped her hands. "Now, children, we are going to sing some nursery rhymes. Sing as loudly as you like, because later, while you are painting, I want you to be as quiet as mice!"

The children gathered round an old piano. Mrs. Fisher played some notes. "One, two, three! Now altogether!" she cried.

At first, Roger hardly dared join in, but he loved nursery rhymes and soon he was singing at the top of his voice.

"That was very nice," said Mrs. Fisher. "Now, off to your tables. Roger, will you sit with Christopher and Lorna, please."

She handed each child a large painting brush and a piece of thick, white paper. Then she put little tins of red, blue, yellow and black paint and a jar of water on every table.

"This morning," she said, "I want you to paint something that you have seen during the weekend."

"I went to the sea," whispered Christopher. "I shall paint that."

"I'm going to paint the swings in the park," said Lorna.

Roger looked at his blank, white paper. He loved painting but he felt uncertain. What *was* he to do?

"I know, I'll paint the red coal truck I saw on Saturday," he decided. He set to work. He was just finishing the last sack of coal, when Mrs. Fisher called:

"Time to stop, children."

She walked slowly round the tables examining every painting carefully. Roger hung his head and stared at his shoes as Mrs. Fisher looked over his shoulder.

As she walked to the Notice Board, all eyes followed her.

"Well, children," she said, "I have enjoyed your work this morning. Bring your paintings to me one at a time, and I will put them up."

The Board was a rainbow of color as the last picture was pinned on it.

"Now," she said, "for the Gold Star. Today, I am going to give it to Roger for a very fine first effort. Well done, Roger!" She stuck a bright, gold star on his painting.

Roger's eyes shone with happiness. "It will soon be time to tell Mom all about it," he thought.

Daniel the Drake and the Magic Frog

This is the story of Daniel, a very dashing young drake who lives on a pond in the middle of a village.

It's a lovely pond, with rushes and reeds and silver birch trees all round it and at one side there's a special place where horses can have a drink if they get thirsty. Daniel looks so warm and happy in his smart clothes, but once upon a time he was the most unhappy little drake there ever was.

One cold winter day, Daniel was swimming round the pond, in and out of the rushes and reeds. He kept looking up at the cold gray sky, just wishing and wishing for the summer to come, so that he could get warm again. Everyone seemed to be warm but Daniel. The village children would come and give him bread and biscuits and once they even brought a piece of birthday cake,

so the young drake was never hungry.

Their red cheeks would glow as they ran about wearing thick woolly mufflers and warm clothes and Daniel loved to watch them playing games and having such fun. He was only poor little Daniel, who sometimes felt so miserable that the tears would roll down his yellow beak and go Plop! into the water.

On that special afternoon, Daniel was feeling very cold and miserable indeed just swimming around, when suddenly he heard a sort of croaky noise. With his sharp black eyes he looked all around, and what do you think he saw? There, by a clump of reeds, sat a poor old frog holding one foot in the air, croaking very loud indeed.

"Hello Mr. Frog," said Daniel, "are you hurt?"

"Hello Daniel," said the frog, "I've hurt my poor foot on a sharp stone and now I can't swim back to my house."

"Never mind," said Daniel, "jump on my back and I'll swim you home in a twinkling."

So the frog jumped on Daniel's back and off they swam. Soon they reached the place where the frog had his home and Daniel was just going to say *Good-by* and *get better soon,* when the frog turned to him and said, "I am a Magic Frog and, because you have been so kind to me, I will grant you a Magic Wish. Choose the thing you want the most, then go to sleep and when you wake up in the morning your wish will have come true."

"Oh," said Daniel, "please could I have something to keep me warm? I do get so cold in the winter. Oh Mr. Frog, I would so like to be warm."

"Of course," said the frog, "off you go now, sleep soundly and in the morning when you wake up you will see that your wish has come true."

So Daniel said *thank you* and *Good night* and swam off feeling very happy and excited.

He dreamt a lovely dream, all about Felicity Fieldmouse, who often came to sit by the side of the pond while she knitted caps and socks for her children. In the dream Felicity was knitting things for Daniel. A white sweater with blue stripes and what else do you think? A lovely cap with a tassel on top.

Early next morning Daniel awoke feeling very cold, and the first thing he saw on the bank by the side of the pond, was a package. Quickly he swam across to have a look. On the top was a big white label with writing

that said: *"A present for Daniel from the Magic Frog".*

Very excited, Daniel untied the string with his beak. The paper fell open and there inside was a white sweater with blue stripes and a lovely cap with a tassel on top. All just like the clothes in his dream!

Shaking the water off his feathers, Daniel jumped out of the water. He put on the clothes. They were a perfect fit, of course, and right away he started to feel warm. Soon he was swimming around the pond singing a song as loud as he could and laughing at the cold gray sky.

Perhaps one day, if you are very lucky, you will go to the village and if you are very lucky indeed, you may see Daniel, swimming around, all dressed up in his sweater and cap.

Mr Gobbledegoop

Mother was peeling and slicing the potatoes for lunch. Rebecca and Giles were helping her.

"Aren't they *huge*!" said Rebecca.

"You can have one each to play with," said Mother.

"What can we do with them?" asked Giles.

"You'll think of something, I'm sure," said Mummy.

Giles found a very funny shaped potato.

"Look, it's just like a man," he said. And he stuck match sticks in the potato to make arms and legs. Then he bent a milk bottle top to make a silvery hat for his little man.

"There," said Giles. "I'm going to call him Mr. Gobbledegoop."

Rebecca wished her potato looked like a little man.

"Never mind," said Mother. "You've got lots of dolls instead."

"But what can I do with my potato?" asked Rebecca.

"Why not make some clothes for Mr. Gobbledegoop?" said Mother.

"But that sounds silly," said Rebecca. "How can you make clothes with a potato?"

"Cut the potato in half, like this," said Mother. "Now use the potato peeler and cut out shapes on the flat side of your potato."

Rebecca thought this was lots of fun, but she still didn't see how she was going to make clothes for Mr. Gobbledegoop.

"Now mix a saucer of paint," said Mother.

Giles mixed one of blue paint and Rebecca mixed a saucer of red paint. And Giles cut out some shapes on the other half of the cut potato.

While they were doing this Mother found a big piece of white cloth. "There now," she said. "Spread the cloth out and you can print pretty patterns all over it."

It was fun! Rebecca printed her red pattern

all over the cloth first, and when it was dry, Giles printed his blue pattern in between the red pattern.

"What a pretty pattern it makes!" they shouted.

"Now what do you think you can do with it?" asked Mother.

"Why, cut out the cloth and make Mr. Gobbledegoop some trousers,' shouted Rebecca.

"And a shirt!" said Giles.

They were busy. Mother helped with the cutting out.

"I can use my toy sewing machine!" said Rebecca.

Soon Mr. Gobbledegoop's suit was ready, and Rebecca carefully put it on the potato man.

He looked so handsome but Rebecca thought he looked lonely.

"Let's make a Mrs. Gobbledegoop," she said. And that's just what they did. And Mrs. Gobbledegoop had a smart potato printed dress too! How they all laughed.

Giles held up Mr. Gobbledegoop and the

potato man bowed to Mrs. Gobbledegoop and said in a funny low voice, "How do you do Mrs. Gobbledegoop. Shall we go for a walk?"

They walked to the window and looked out and had a funny gobbledegoop conversation, watching all the people go by.

Wouldn't you like to make a Gobbledegoop family one day?

The Goldfish

Around his bowl the goldfish swims,
With great big eyes and golden fins,
He hasn't very much to do,
Except look out and see the view.
I wonder why he grins and grins?
When all he does is swims and swims.

Dancing Pins

Simon's Auntie owned a little dress shop in the High Street. And sometimes Mother left Simon with his Auntie while she went to do her shopping. Simon loved helping Auntie. But the thing he liked best was when Auntie made the pins dance.

"Make the pins dance and stand up," he used to say. And Auntie would put some pins on a piece of paper. Then she moved her hand under the paper and the pins jumped up and moved about all over the paper. But when Simon put his hand under the paper, the pins would not dance for him.

One day Simon sat and watched as Auntie was shortening a dress for a lady. It was a beautiful dress, but it was much too long. The lady stood very still and very straight. Auntie knelt down and began to pin up the dress. She had a big fat pincushion strapped to her wrist like a bracelet where she kept the pins. Auntie's mouth

was full of pins too. When Auntie talked, Simon hoped and hoped she would not swallow any pins. On the table behind, there was a box full of pins too. And there were pins on the floor too. In fact there were pins everywhere.

"There," said Auntie in a funny voice because her mouth was full of pins. "Walk over there and let's see if the hem is even."

Auntie got up quickly and knocked the box of pins off the table. They spilled all over the carpet.

"I'll pick them up," said Simon. And he started picking them up, one by one. It was such a long job. Auntie was too busy with the lady to think about the pins. But when the lady had gone out of the shop, Auntie said, "I've got a much quicker way of picking up pins. Look, use this!"

And she held out a huge magnet. "Just run this along the carpet and it will even pick up the ones that you cannot see."

It was such fun. The pins jumped to the magnet and all bunched together at the end

of it. He soon picked up all the pins.

"Now we pull them off the magnet and pop them back in the box," said Auntie.

"Is *that* how you make the pins dance?" asked Simon; he suddenly understood how Auntie had made them dance.

"Yes, you've discovered the secret at last," Auntie laughed.

Simon spent the rest of the morning picking up pins in all sorts of corners of the shop, and at the back of Auntie's needle and cotton cupboard. It was such fun. He

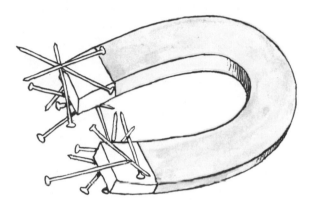

went round the shop to find out what else the magnet would pull towards it. The magnet hung from the door handle and it was even strong enough to pull Auntie's scissors across the table. He soon found that the magnet would not pull anything but iron.

"Try pulling this along," said Auntie. And she took a ring off her finger.

"It doesn't work," said Simon.

"That's because the ring is made of real gold," said Auntie.

When it was time to go home, Simon showed Mother the huge magnet.

"Simon has been such a good boy this morning," said Auntie. "He has picked up all the pins all over the floor. I think he should be rewarded for his work. There you are," she said and she gave Simon the magnet as a reward.

"Oh, thank you, Auntie," said Simon.

"But you must bring it every time you come and pick up my pins," said Auntie.

"Yes, and I'll make the pins dance for *you,*" said Simon.

The Wonder of Nature

Flowers grow
All by themselves
Without the help
Of fairies or elves.

Plants and food
The farmer sows,
What makes them tasty
Nobody knows.

The Grumpy Red Bus

The red bus was feeling grumpy. It was because it was raining.

Now some people love the rain. They love to go 'splash, splash' through the puddles. But not the red bus. He hated splashing through the puddles and making his beautiful red coat all muddy.

"I'm not going out today," he said to himself when Jack his driver came into the garage.

"Come along now, what's the matter this morning, got the grumps?" asked Jack as he tried to start him up.

"Grurr," said the red bus. Or something that sounded like that.

But he had to go because Jack kept prodding and poking him about so much that he couldn't stand it in the end.

"That's better then," said Jack as they set off down the road.

"Is it then," grumbled the red bus to himself. "Any moment now I shall hear that conductor ring his bell and I'll be jerked up so suddenly that my inside will rattle.

"And then people will start crowding inside me and when I am full and Jim can't reach his bell, he'll stamp down his great heavy feet. It's not nice to treat me like that. How would he like to be stamped on if he were all filled up inside?"

And so the red bus grumbled on. He was so busy grumbling that he didn't even notice that he hadn't been stopped until they reached the Town Hall.

Standing on the steps of the Town Hall were lots of children with buckets and spades. "Hurray," they all shouted when they saw the red bus.

"Goodness, they're cheering me!" cried the red bus with surprise.

40

Then the children clambered into the red bus, still cheering and waving their buckets and spades. They climbed all over the seats and they stamped their feet on the floor. But somehow the red bus didn't seem to mind the children stamping their feet.

Actually he rather liked it. Because they seemed to beat a cheerful tune, "tappity tap, tappity tap." And he tried to sing a cheerful tune. "Burr burr burr," he sang as he sped along the road.

Along the country lanes they sped, never stopping until they reached the seaside.

It wasn't raining at the seaside. The sun was shining and the sky was blue.

"Hurray," shouted the children as they climbed out of the red bus and raced down to the beach.

The children had a lovely picnic on the beach. The red bus had a picnic too, with some seagulls. They brought bits of bread and had a picnic on his roof. The red bus said "Stay as long as you like," but the sea-

gulls flew away when the children came back.

What strange things they brought back with them! Lumps of seaweed, winkles and sand.

They spilled some of the sand from their buckets and it trickled through some cracks in the floor boards.

It tickled the red bus and he cried "haw-haw." But the children didn't hear him because they were all laughing so loudly.

They laughed and sang all the way home. And so did Jack and Jim, and so did the little red bus.

He was still singing softly to himself when at last Jack put him away in his garage. What a lovely day it had been!

41

Dumpling the Cuddly Hedgehog

It sounds very funny to talk about a cuddly hedgehog, when everybody knows that you can't cuddle something all covered in prickles. But, Dumpling is different—instead of having hard spines, he has soft ones—so he really is a cuddly hedgehog.

When he first knew he was different, he was very unhappy. The other little hedgehogs wouldn't play with him; they would tease him and chase him and make him very miserable. It wasn't very kind of them, was it?

One day he had a long, long think and he decided what to do. He decided to run away.

Early next morning, Dumpling woke up, washed his face and set out down the lane and through the hedge. He found beech nuts and water for breakfast and he felt very happy indeed. All that day he was walking and playing little games by himself.

The time soon passed and as the sun began to go down, he started feeling tired and to realize that he had no idea at all where he was going to sleep. He was also very hungry as well and a nice dinner was something he wanted very much.

Just as the first star twinkled in the sky, Dumpling saw a little house by the side of the wood, and though his tired legs were very slow he got there somehow. Dumpling didn't know much about houses, but he did know that you had to go through the door to get inside. But he was so little, he couldn't reach the knob or the knocker. It began to get cold and poor Dumpling just sat on the mat and looked at the door, wondering what to do.

Inside the little house Bessie Hedgehog was getting the supper ready while her sister Minnie lit the lamp and set out spoons and bowls, mugs and plates, honey and cream, on the nice white table cloth.

It was cozy in the cottage, the fire burned brightly and the lamp glowed soft and yellow on the dresser and a most delicious smell came from the kitchen.

Soon, the supper was ready and Bessie and Minnie sat down at the table. To begin with they each had a large bowl of warm bread and milk with lots of honey, then a lovely apple dumpling all soft and golden inside a light and fluffy crust.

"Have some more dumpling, Minnie," said Bessie.

mat was a tiny baby hedgehog, the smallest you have ever seen. There he was, shivering with the cold, his two little black eyes streaming with tears. He did look miserable.

"Oh, poor little thing!" said Minnie, "come along now, don't cry any more."

So she picked him up, wrapped him up in a blanket and put him in a basket near the fire. Bessie brought him some warm bread and milk, but he didn't eat very much of that. So they gave him a dish of apple dumpling and do you know what he did? He ate up all the dumpling, every bit, then he

"No thank you, dear," said her sister, "I've had such a big supper, I really couldn't manage another crumb."

So, they both had their cocoa and then sat by the fire. Minnie suddenly jumped, when she heard a loud sneezy noise.

"Oh Bessie," she said, "have you caught a cold?"

"No," said her sister.

"But I just heard a sneeze: who could it be?"

So they both listened and then they heard a loud sneeze and this time, a sob as well.

"Oh dear," said Bessie, "there's somebody outside our front door, sneezing and crying, whoever can it be?"

So together, they opened the door and looked out and there all curled up on the

held out the bowl for some more. Bessie and Minnie laughed, but they filled the bowl again and soon the baby had eaten it all up.

"Well I never," said Bessie, "he really likes dumpling; he's eaten so much he looks a bit like a dumpling himself. I think we'll call him that until we find out his name."

Dumpling loved it in the little house. Nobody ever teased him or chased him again and they all lived happily ever after.

The Little Church

Mother couldn't tell Katie her usual bed-time story because she had to go out. So Daddy said: "I'll tell you a story instead. What shall it be about?"

"We often have stories about a mouse, or a kitten or a pony," said Katie. "So could we have a story about something different?"

"Well, what do you want it to be about tonight?" asked Daddy.

Katie thought hard. "About a . . . about a . . ." but she couldn't think.

"Hurry up," said Daddy, "or your story-time will be over. We've only got two minutes, don't forget."

Katie thought very hard. "About a . . . about a . . . *church*!" she said quickly.

"Oh, that's difficult," said Daddy. "Churches are particularly difficult to tell a story about. Why don't you start it and I'll finish it for you?" he suggested.

"Once upon a time . . ." started Katie. "There was a little old church . . . I can't think of any more," she said.

"Well, I'll finish it," said Daddy (who was very clever at finishing other people's stories). "Once upon a time there was a little old church and it stood right at the top of a hill. It had stood there for years and years. But, of course, no one visited it except on Sunday mornings. Do you know why no one went there in the evenings?" asked Daddy.

"No," said Katie.

"Because the little church was so far away from anywhere that there was no electricity or gas—it had no lights at all. And it was a very, very long climb to the church. And Mr. Pooks who used to carry coal or oil for the lamps was too old to do it any more.

" 'We stopped having church services up at the church for years now,' " he said.

"Now the rector's little girl was called—

shall we call her Katie?" asked Daddy.

"Yes!" shouted Katie.

"Katie wanted to have carol-singing on Christmas Eve at the church, so she thought and thought how they could light that little church, so that the people could sing carols without sitting in the dark.

"At last she had a wonderful idea.

"She wrote a big notice and asked her Daddy if she could hang it in the church porch. The notice said:

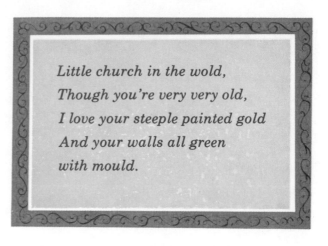

Little church in the wold,
Though you're very very old,
I love your steeple painted gold
And your walls all green
with mould.

CAROL SINGING

ON CHRISTMAS EVE

BRING YOUR OWN CANDLE

"So on Christmas Eve all the people climbed up the hill to the little church and when they arrived in the porch, Katie's Daddy stood at the door and he lit everyone's candle. Then they went in and sat down. The more people who went into the church, the lighter and lighter and brighter the church grew, until it was like the blazing stars in the sky. It was so exciting.

"And it was the loveliest Christmas carol-singing anyone ever remembered. And, do you know, they always do that every Christmas now. Wasn't Katie's idea a clever one?"

Cowslip Keys

One afternoon Jenny and Mother went up on the hills to look for cowslips. Up and up they climbed to the very top, but they only found one cowslip.

"Never mind," said Mother. "I expect there will be plenty more soon. Let's sit down and look at the view."

"Yes," said Jenny. "And I will tell you a story."

Jenny loved to make up stories for Mother. "I will tell you one about this cowslip," she said.

"Now this cowslip is not an ordinary cowslip. It's really a gold key."

"That's interesting," said Mother.

"Yes," said Jenny. "This cowslip key belongs to a lady mole, who owns the cowslip stores inside this hill. She has lost this key and can't unlock her door until she finds it, so I shall give it to her when she comes looking for it.

"Ah, here she comes now. Can you see her, Mother?"

Mother didn't answer. She had closed her eyes as if she were asleep.

So Jenny waited for the mole to come up close and then she held out the cowslip key.

"Thank you," said the mole. "Would you like to come and see my cowslip stores."

Jenny was delighted. She jumped up and followed the mole down the side of the hill as far as a little blue door which was half hidden beneath a yellow gorse bush.

The mole opened the door with her cowslip key and they went inside.

Everywhere was lit up with tiny glowworm lanterns which were hung all round the walls. There were shelves all round the walls and they were crowded with the strangest assortment of objects.

All muddled up with pots of honey, wild raspberry jam and blackberry jelly were spider spun shawls and green and purple gloves.

"Come and visit me any time you like," said the mole. "Take the key."

"I promise not to lose it," said Jenny.

"That's all right. There will be plenty of cowslips out soon," said the mole. "They all fit this lock you know."

"Cowslips really *are* gold keys," said Jenny as she sat down once more on the hill beside Mother.

"Yes dear, so you said. Is there any more to the story?" asked Mother opening her eyes.

She stared at Jenny. "Are you asleep?" she asked.

"Of course not," said Jenny. "I just closed my eyes to think. There's so much to tell you and I have to sort it out a bit."

"Why, they're made from foxgloves," cried Jenny as she picked up a pair and tried them on.

"Yes, Mrs. Fox makes them. She brings them in every morning," said the mole. "And Mr. Toad brings those stools over there."

She pointed to a heap of toadstools in a corner.

"Mrs. Frog brings those mats made from bullrushes. I believe she sits by the pond and makes them."

"Who brings the acorn cups and walnut bowls?" asked Jenny.

"Mr. Squirrel, of course," said the mole. "He collects quite a lot of nuts for storing away during the winter. So in the spring he has a lot of shells to bring me. We animals are always busy you know; we work hard when we're awake, to make up for the time we lose when we're asleep."

"Yes," said Jenny. Talking of sleep reminded her of Mother. "I must go now," she told the mole.

Lost in the Jungle

It is not nice to be lost in the jungle and young Zoë, the zebra, was lost indeed.

"I wish I hadn't stopped to play with you," she said to the family of baboons who squatted around her.

"Well, if you hadn't fallen asleep under that tree, you would never have been left behind," said an old baboon.

"But I was so hot and tired, and *now* I'm very thirsty!" said Zoë.

The baboon scratched his head. "I heard the zebras say they were going down to the river to drink," he said. "We will go with you part of the way in case you get lost."

"Oh, thank you!" cried Zoë and, surrounded by chattering baboons she set off.

No sooner had they disappeared through the long grass, than a lioness and her three cubs stalked up and settled themselves under the shade of the tree.

But unaware of the danger they had been in, Zoë trotted along with her new friends.

"We shall soon reach the main track down to the drinking place," said the old baboon, "and there we must leave you."

At that moment, there was a loud trumpeting sound and the ground shook. The baboons became very excited.

"The elephants are going to the river!" they cried. "You must go with them."

An old elephant, wrinkled and creased, led the herd of great beasts. He lowered his huge head and looked at Zoë and the baboons.

"Go on, ask him if he will take you with them," whispered the old baboon.

Zoë gazed up at the old elephant. "I fell asleep," she said timidly, "and my family have gone to the drinking place without me. May I go with you to the river, please?"

The old elephant swished his trunk. "Of course you may," he said kindly. "You will be safe with us. Come!"

So Zoë said good-by to the baboons and trotted away, keeping close to the elephant.

Soon the track widened into a meadow and there lay the river, shining under the hot sun. Gazelles were eating the soft grass by the water—but there were no zebras.

"Oh, dear," cried Zoë, "what shall I do? I really *am* lost!"

"Don't worry," said the old elephant, "hippopotamus sees everyone who comes down to the river. While you have a drink, we will ask him if he has seen your family!"

As the elephants walked into the shallow water near the river bank, the water swirled and up popped hippopotamus, his great body shining and his small eyes gleaming with curiosity.

"Hello," grunted hippopotamus. "Who's that with you?"

The old elephant swished some water over himself. "It's young zebra; she has lost her family. We thought they might be here."

Hippopotamus opened his huge mouth and yawned lazily.

"Well, they *have* been here, but they were scared by a tiger and rushed off with the giraffes not long ago. If she hurried she'd probably catch them up."

"I see she has made some new friends," said the old elephant, looking across at Zoë.

The little zebra was busy telling the gazelles of her troubles.

"We are just leaving, why don't you come with us?" they said.

As the gazelles turned away from the water, Zoë turned with them.

"Good-by!" trumpeted the elephants.

Swiftly, the graceful gazelles and Zoë sped on.

"Do you think we might catch up with my family before night comes?" asked Zoë.

Before anyone could answer her, a giraffe raced across the track. He stopped and bent his long neck to look at Zoë.

"Have you been lost all day?" he asked.

"Yes, I have. I've . . ."

"Well, your mother is waiting for you through those trees. We've been looking for you everywhere!" interrupted the giraffe.

Happily, and without another word, the little zebra raced through the trees, to her mother!

Moving House

"Your father is quite right, children, we shall have to move." Mrs. Sparrow settled herself on the house gutter and watched a golden leaf flutter by. "Our home at the top of this drainpipe has been very nice, but we need somewhere sheltered and warm now that Autumn is here."

Sydney, who had been the first of the sparrow children to hatch that Spring and was a handsome, dark feathered young bird, puffed out his chest. "Where is father, anyway?" he chirped.

"I haven't seen him since breakfast," said his young sister, Sally, fluttering her pale brown feathers.

"He has gone to the bakery in town to see if there is room for us there," replied Mrs Sparrow. "It would be nice to smell fresh bread every day and I hear the baker is very generous with crumbs."

"I don't *want* to move away," grumbled Sydney.

"Neither do I," cheeped Sally, "I love this house and garden and I like the family who live here. The children put down bread for us and the corn they throw out for the white pigeons is absolutely delicious."

"Yes," shouted Sydney very crossly and loudly, "Sally and I *won't* move, so there.

Come on, Sal!" and that rude little sparrow flew off into an oak tree.

"*Please* don't move away," cried Sally and, giving Mrs. Sparrow a soft peck, she flew after Sydney, almost colliding with a house martin on the way.

"Anyone would think those house martins owned the place," said Sydney. "They zoom around catching flies all the time and look at all the nests they have."

"Yes," answered Sally "I heard one of the children say he had counted forty martins' houses stuck to the walls under the eaves.

They may be bossy, but they are clever and very handsome."

"No *wonder* there's no room for us," grunted Sydney and the two sparrows watched as the martins flashed about the sky with their little forked tails, white chests and glossy black backs.

"Thank goodness *that* lot will soon be gone," said a harsh voice from a branch above the sparrows, and a large jackdaw hopped down beside them. "Can't stand the cold, they can't; they'll be off to find the sun any time now and we'll have the garden to ourselves again. They'll be back next Spring, though—use the same nests year after year. I'll say this for them, they are good builders —marvellous things their mud nests."

"Sally!" shouted Sydney "I've got a wonderful idea! Why don't *we* borrow one of their nests for the winter and give it back to them in the Spring?"

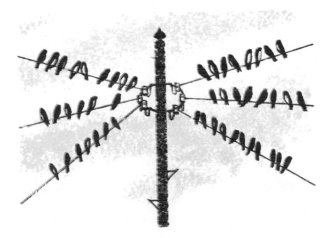

The Circus

Roll up and see the Circus,
Cries the man in the shiney hat,
Roll up and see the animals,
And the wonderful way they act.

We have lions, we have horses,
And a very funny clown,
Who tries to climb up to the roof,
And then comes tumbling down.

"Um," grunted the jackdaw, "you'll have to get out pretty quickly when the martins come back or there will be trouble, but I don't mind keeping a look out for you."

"We could move back to the drainpipe in the Spring," chirruped Sally. "Let's fly and tell mother!"

They found Mr. and Mrs. Sparrow looking very gloomy. "No room at the bakery, it's full of town sparrows," said Mr. Sparrow.

Squeaking with excitement Sydney and Sally explained their Plan. When the sparrow parents realized that such an important bird as Jackdaw was willing to help them, they happily agreed.

The very next week all the martins gathered on a telegraph wire early one morning and before lunchtime they had all flown away.

Eagerly the sparrow family flew round the house looking for just the right martin's nest to borrow. They found a large one stuck to the wall under the roof eaves, just like a mud sack with a hole in the top. All through the winter they were warm and snug and as Spring drew near again, they knew that Jackdaw in his nest in the chimney would give them good warning of the returning martins.

The Football Match

James wanted to be a football player when he grew up. He watched the football match every Saturday—but not with the crowd who paid to go in because James couldn't afford to pay.

James had a secret way of watching. He had found a little hole in the fence at just the right height for himself, and he peeped through that. Of course, he couldn't watch all the game—only when the players came to the goal at his end of the field.

One Saturday he was watching the match as usual when Bert, the carpenter, came along.

"Hello, who's winning?" asked Bert.

"I don't know," said James. "The team in the red shirts seem to be very good because they are always near the goal at the other end of the field this week. I can't see them through this hole when they are playing at the other end."

"Well," said Bert. "Shall I drill a hole for you with my big drill?" He bent down and started to open his tool kit to find the drill.

"Oh, no," said James, a little frightened. He knew that wouldn't be at all right. "You can't drill holes in other people's fences!"

"Perhaps you're right, but I tell you what," said Bert. "I know quite a lot about wood. Let me show you something. Have you ever heard of knots?"

"The knots they learn in Boy Scouts?" asked James.

"No, knots in wood are different," laughed Bert. "Come and look here. Every piece of wood has long lines in it—that's called the grain. But every now and then you find a little circle of hard wood. That's called a knot in the wood. Look, there's one." He pointed to a circle in the wood.

"Now do you know what that knot was when this piece of wood was a tree?"

"No," said James.

"A branch grew out of that knot once!" said Bert, proudly.

"Oh," said James. But he did not understand how that was going to help him see the football match.

"Now," said Bert mysteriously. "When a fence is old and dry, the wood shrinks and that little circle of wood sometimes—only sometimes, mind you—falls out, leaving a hole for young boys like you to peep through. Let's look for one near the other end, shall we?"

They looked and looked. James found one. He pressed his finger gently into the knot and the little circle of wood fell out!

"There, what did I tell you?" said Bert and off he went, whistling happily.

So now James ran from one hole to the other watching the football players as they moved from one end of the field to the other.

Suddenly the football came whizzing right over the top of the fence. James ran to pick it up, but he was not big enough to throw the ball back again.

James and the Captain talked through one of James' little knot holes.

"Can you bring the ball round to the gates?" asked the Captain.

Proudly James carried the big ball under his arm and marched up to the gate-keeper.

"This little fellow saved our ball for us," said the Captain. "I think he deserves to be allowed to come in and watch the rest of the match."

The gate-keeper let James in and, for the first time, James watched the match in the best seats.

At the end of the match the Captain came and lifted James up on his shoulders and gave him a ride through the crowds!

But James still watched the football match from his little knot holes every Saturday after that!

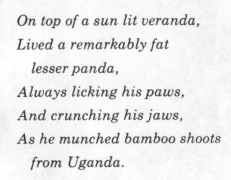

On top of a sun lit veranda,
Lived a remarkably fat
  lesser panda,
Always licking his paws,
And crunching his jaws,
As he munched bamboo shoots
  from Uganda.

Gretchen,
the little Dutch doll

Gretchen, the little Dutch doll belonged to Mandy. But Mandy was such a careless girl and whenever she dropped anything she never bothered to pick it up, she just left it—even Gretchen.

This made Gretchen cross. She liked to keep her white cap and apron nice and clean. And she didn't like her blue and white dress to get too creased. Nor did she like to get mud on her white shoes. And certainly not on her pretty pink cheeks.

But it didn't worry Mandy. She'd take poor Gretchen into the garden, drop her down and leave her there, sometimes flat on her back with her legs stuck up in the air.

"How would she like to be left out like this?" grumbled Gretchen to herself, when no one was around to hear.

Once Mandy left her in the garden and it began to rain. Luckily, Rags the puppy saw her and carried her indoors.

Gretchen thought it was kind of him but she wished he hadn't dropped her into Mrs. Cat's basket.

Mrs. Cat was very kind. She let Gretchen share the cushion in her basket. She treated her just like one of her own kittens. As soon as Mrs. Cat had gone to sleep Gretchen slipped quietly out of the basket.

She slid across the kitchen floor to the chair by the window. Luckily for her, someone had knocked the tea-cozy on to the floor and not noticed it. So she crawled under the chair and pulled the tea-cozy over her for the night.

She felt safe there from everybody.

She must have slept well because when she woke up in the morning she could hear the family having breakfast.

But Mandy didn't want any breakfast.

"I want my Gretchen," she kept saying. "Boo, hoo, I don't want any breakfast, I want my Gretchen."

Gretchen was surprised to hear how much Mandy loved her.

She thought perhaps she'd better come out from under the tea-cozy.

Mandy's Mother said, "If you weren't so careless, Mandy, and treated Gretchen better you wouldn't lose her. However, I don't suppose she's far away. I'm sure we'll find her after breakfast."

Just then Rags, the puppy, saw Gretchen and he barked. That made Mother and Mandy look under the chair.

The Toy Train

Toy train Timmy
Chugging round the track,
No sooner here
Than he's going back.

Puffing past the signals,
Hooting at the signs,
Timmy's very happy
He's on the railway lines!

"Oh, there she is. There's my dear little Gretchen," cried Mandy picking her up and giving her a big kiss and a hug.

"Fancy that," said Mother. "She was hiding under my tea-cozy."

Mandy took great care of Gretchen after that. She cleaned the doll's face and hands and washed and ironed her clothes and never left her out in the rain again.

She even took her to bed with her just to make sure she was safe at night.

And Gretchen thought Mandy must be the nicest little girl in the world, and she loved her ever after.

Busy Timmy Tug

The big ocean liner was impatient to be off on her voyage round the world. She felt just as excited as her passengers, for she had never been all round the world before.

"I wish they'd hurry up and come aboard," she said to herself. "I wish they'd pull up the gangways and start up my engines."

"Hello," called Timmy Tug, as he darted by.

The big liner didn't answer. She felt much too grand to talk to tiny tugs. "Silly little things," she muttered. "Always bustling here, there and everywhere."

"Hello," called Timmy Tug again, as he darted back. "We'll soon be off now, I'm nearly ready."

"Huh," muttered the big liner. "Does he think he's coming with me? Huh."

"Back in a minute," called Timmy Tug, as he bustled by once more.

"Don't bother yourself," said the big liner. "I'll be leaving any minute now."

Sure enough, it did look as if all the passengers had come aboard for the gangways were being removed.

"Hurrah, now perhaps they will start up my engines," cried the big liner.

She loved the thump-thump of her big powerful engines. They made her feel as though she could cut the waves in half. Just slice them through—like that. And what a lovely 'wash' she made as she cut through the water.

Ah, she was moving. But what was that moving along with her? Pulling her?

Goodness, it was that silly little tug. Did they really think he was going to pull her out to sea?

She was cross. She felt so silly being pulled along by a tiny tug. Was there something wrong with her? Was that little tug going to pull her all round the world?

Then she heard a sailor talking to some children. "Useful little things, tugs," he said. "We couldn't get in or out of the harbor without them."

"Why not?" asked a small boy.

"Because our engines are too powerful," said the sailor. "We'd set up such a 'wash' that we'd swamp everybody in the harbor. We'd be in real disgrace then."

"Oh," murmured the liner softly. "I hadn't thought of that."

She didn't want to be in disgrace for upsetting other people, oh dear no. And she began to be thankful to the tug for saving her from doing so.

So she said "thank you" very politely to Timmy Tug when at last they reached the open sea.

"It was a pleasure," said Timmy Tug. "I hope you will have a lovely voyage."

"How kind of you," shouted back the liner. She had to shout because her engines were whirring and making such a noise. And Timmy Tug moved so quickly he was already half-way back to the wharf.

"I hope we will meet again when I come home," called the liner.

They did. Timmy Tug was there to pull her back into the harbor. She wanted to tell him all her adventures but he was too busy to stop long enough to hear them.

But when his work was finished for the day he managed to slip alongside her and whisper; "Now tell me all about your adventures."

So they talked together under the stars, the big liner and Timmy Tug. When they'd finished talking Timmy Tug looked up at her and said respectfully, "You must feel very grand."

"No," said the big liner. "I don't." And she meant it. "Without your help, Timmy Tug, I could never have started on my adventures," she said.

And she was right, wasn't she?

The lucky Donkey

Dolly, the donkey was tired of her job. It was not very interesting pulling a junkman's cart round the streets all day long. And not very pleasant in the winter, when it was wet. If there was one thing Dolly disliked more than anything else it was getting her feet wet. However loaded her cart was, she would step to one side rather than walk through a puddle.

Then one day, something happened to brighten Dolly's dull life. A new family moved into the big white house she passed every morning.

There was a little boy in the family called Andy. He quickly made friends with Dolly.

He was playing in the garden when he first saw her. "Look at that lovely donkey, Mother," he shouted as Dolly came along the street.

Dolly was surprised to hear him call out. She stopped by the gate and peered through at him. Nobody had ever called her a lovely donkey before. Because she wasn't really a lovely donkey.

She was too thin, and her coat wasn't well groomed because Mick her master was always too tired at the end of the day to bother much with her. So after she'd had her supper he always hurried off to get his supper.

Still, to young Andy, she was lovely.

"Let's give her something to eat," he said to his mother.

Mick said Dolly liked thistles. "We have plenty of them in the garden," laughed Andy's mother.

They picked her some thistles and Dolly ate every one.

"Good-by, we'll give you some more tomorrow," called Andy when Mick said they must be "getting along" now.

From then on Dolly looked forward to

stopping by the gate of the big white house, and having her lunch of thistles.

Even if it was raining Andy would be watching at the window and would run out with a big umbrella over his head and a bunch of thistles in his hand. "Here's your lunch, Dolly," he'd call as he ran down the path.

Then one day Mick had some sad news for Andy.

"I'm giving up work because I'm too old," he told him. "So I shall have to sell Dolly."

Andy was upset. "Could we buy Dolly?" he asked his daddy that evening.

"We have nowhere to keep her," said his daddy. "Our garden is not big enough."

"Uncle Jim has plenty of room on his farm," said Andy. "He could keep her there and we could see her on weekends."

Daddy said he'd think about it.

He did think about it. And he did more than that. He went to see Uncle Jim who had lots of room on his farm for a donkey. And Uncle Jim said the donkey could come and live in one of his fields. So daddy bought Dolly.

Everyone was delighted. Mick was pleased because he knew Dolly was going to a good home. Dolly was excited when she arrived on the farm and saw the lovely green field and her comfortable little donkey shed.

And Andy was glad that he'd thought about it because he was able to learn to ride Dolly round the field.

Every weekend he came to ride her. "I hope you are not lonely when we're not here," he'd say to her.

How could she ever be lonely—on a farm?

When Andy was not with her she had chickens to keep her company. And ducks waddling about in her field.

And cows calling over the hedge. She could never be lonely.

"I'm a lucky donkey," she'd keep saying to herself.

And she was a lovely donkey too. Because she was not thin any more. And her coat was always well-groomed. Andy saw to that— with the help of Uncle Jim.

✳✳✳✳✳✳✳✳✳✳✳✳✳✳

This is the story of Tommy White,
Who didn't know his left hand from his right.
He pushed a lever inside his truck,
Pushed it so hard that it stuck.
The back of his truck went down THUD!
And covered his friend all over, with mud!

✳✳✳✳✳✳✳✳✳✳✳✳✳✳

Joey knew best

Mrs. Buffles had a parrot—a little green parrot called Joey which she kept in her greenhouse next to the kitchen. Mrs. Buffles spent a lot of time in the greenhouse, busy amongst her flowerpots planting bulbs and seeds.

One day Jill and Giles were with her and she let them talk to Joey. Joey said: "Pretty polly, pretty polly!" and sometimes other things like: "Close the door!"

"May I feed him?" asked Jill.

"Yes," said Mrs. Buffles. And she gave Jill some bird seed.

"Is bird seed real seed?" asked Giles. "I mean, if I plant it, will it grow?"

"Yes, of course," said Mrs. Buffles.

"I'd love to grow some" said Jill.

"Then you shall have some," said Mrs. Buffles.

"May I have some too?" asked Giles.

"Yes," said Mrs. Buffles. "And I will give a prize to the one who grows the tallest plant."

"Oh, then may I choose one that's *not* in Joey's bowl?" asked Giles.

"Which would you like?" asked Mrs. Buffles.

"That big bulb over there," said Giles.

"Greedy lad! Greedy lad!" said the parrot.

Jill chose some small striped seeds from Joey's bowl.

And when they went home, they planted their seeds and the bulbs in the little patch of garden outside the kitchen door. They watered them and looked after them for such a long time before anything happened. Then Giles' started showing first. "I knew I would win," said Giles, "because I chose the biggest."

At last Jill's seed started sprouting and soon it was quite an exciting race as Jill's starting catching up with Giles', then Jill's plant was exactly the same height as Giles', and then it grew *taller* than Giles' plant.

Giles measured his plant every day. It grew to about two feet and soon a yellow flower burst out of its sheath.

"It's a daffodil!" said Giles.

Jill's plant went on growing and growing, but it didn't show any flower for a long time. Giles' flower looked lovely but the plant stopped growing any taller.

Jill had to push a stick into the ground to tie her plant and stop it from flopping over. Up, up, up went the plant and then at last a flower appeared. The flower grew and grew; it was yellow too, with a brown center. The size of the flower was first as big as a saucer, then as big as a little plate, then it grew to the size of a large dinner plate. Jill had to stand on a stool to measure her plant now, and the big flower kept turning towards the sun.

"It's a sunflower," said Mother.

At last Mrs. Buffles came round to see who was the winner. She brought Joey with her on her shoulder.

"Jill is the winner," she said.

"But I chose the *biggest* to begin with," said Giles, crossly.

"Greedy lad, greedy lad," said the parrot.

"Perhaps Joey is right," said Mrs. Buffles. "The biggest thing does not always turn out the biggest in the end. And when Jill's flower has finished blooming, the centre will be full of more sunflower seeds for Joey's breakfast. You must save them for him!"

And do you know what Mrs. Buffles did? She bought the seeds from Jill—that was Jill's prize!

Surprise for Victoria

Victoria lived in an old house in the country. It had low beamed ceilings, large cozy fireplaces *and* creaking floorboards.

Victoria loved her home—she even loved its noisy floorboards and when the house creaked at night, she snuggled down in bed, imagining the house was talking to her.

She often wondered, too, about the people who had lived in the house before her mother and father had come to live there, and where she and her baby brother, James, had both been born.

"Our house is very old, isn't it, Mother?" Victoria asked one day. "How long have there been people living in it?"

"Yes it is *very* old, dear. Lots of families have lived here for over three hundred years," said her mother.

Victoria opened her eyes very wide. "I wonder if there has always been a child sleeping in my bedroom," she said.

"I am sure there has been!" said mother.

"Do you think that a child who lived here long, long ago would have been very different from me?" enquired Victoria.

"Well, she would have worn very different clothes," replied mother, "but there would be a little girl very much like you inside them. I expect she liked playing with dolls

Butterflies

Butterflies have painted wings,
With eyes on stalks,
And legs like strings.

You can see them,
Come and go,
Fluttering in the Summer glow.

From flower to flower,
They love to play,
But only live for one whole day.

and dressing up and having tea parties, just like you do."

"I'm glad!" laughed Victoria.

That evening, as her father bent over her bed to wish her goodnight, a floorboard gave a very loud squeak.

"Dear, oh dear," said father. "What a noise your floor makes! I must have a look at it tomorrow."

"*I* don't mind the squeaks, daddy," murmured Victoria and fell fast asleep. She dreamt about another little girl who had lived in her home many, many years before, and the funny thing was that her name was Victoria, too!

The next morning Victoria's father said: "Let's go and see if I can stop that floor of yours creaking."

Hand in hand they climbed the old staircase to Victoria's room. They rolled back the carpet by her bed and her father looked at the polished floor carefully.

"Ah!" he exclaimed, "*here's* the loose board." And he was able to lift it easily.

"There's quite a lot of space underneath the floor, isn't there?" said Victoria, leaning over his shoulder.

"Yes, there is—do you know, I think there's something hidden down there!"

"Daddy, daddy! What is it? What is it?" Victoria squealed.

Carefully, her father drew something out. At first, Victoria could not make out what it was—it was so very dirty.

"Why, it's a doll!" she cried, as the dust was gently brushed away.

"And a very old one, too," said her father, "I wonder how long it's been there."

Victoria stared at the doll. She saw two bright blue eyes staring back at *her* from a dainty china face; she saw that the rest of the doll's body was made of painted wood and she saw that its dress had once been a very old fashioned pretty muslin with flowers on it and it was trimmed with lace.

"I think she's *beautiful*," whispered Victoria. "I wonder who she belonged to?"

"To another little girl who loved her very much, I expect," said mother who had just come into the room.

Victoria smiled. "And I shall love her just the same," she said.

"What will you call her?" asked her mother.

"Victoria!" said Victoria.

"But why call her the same name as yourself?" asked her mother.

"Because I think I dreamt about her last night and her name was Victoria in my dream!" said Victoria.

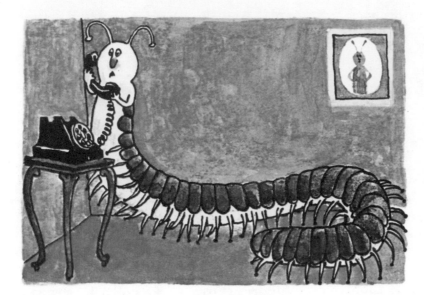

Charlie Centipede

Charlie Centipede had a hundred feet. That's why he was called 'centipede'—which means a hundred feet.

Some people might find having a hundred feet useful. Not Charlie. He thought they were a nuisance.

The trouble was he kept getting them wet. And then he'd have a cold.

Once he had such a bad cold that he telephoned for Doctor Dormouse to come and look at him.

Doctor Dormouse put Charlie's feet into a hot mustard bath—all one hundred of them. There wasn't much to see of Charlie while he was in the bath. Just his head poking up above the water. But Doctor Dormouse said it would do him a lot of good.

Then he dried him and put him to bed.

While he was in bed, he thought about his friend, Harry Horse. Now Harry never caught a cold. Perhaps it was because he wore shoes. So he never had wet feet.

So as soon as he was well, he wrapped a warm scarf round his neck and off he went to the shoe shop.

"What size shoes would you like?" asked the shopkeeper.

"Size fifty," said Charlie.

"Size fifty," cried the shopkeeper. "I've never heard of that size, you'll need to get them specially made. Why do you want such big ones?"

"Well," said Charlie. "It's like this. I have one hundred feet. Now it would be too expensive to buy fifty pairs of shoes, but if I could get one big pair of shoes, I could put fifty feet into each shoe, see?"

The shopkeeper was not sure about that. However as he hadn't any big enough shoes he offered Charlie a big pair of heavy snow boots.

Charlie slipped one on. Or rather, he slipped into one, right to the bottom, and the shopkeeper had to lift him out with a button hook. Charlie *was* upset.

"It's no use, I shall have to get some specially made," he said. And off he went.

On the way home he met his friend, Harry Horse. Harry told him he always had his shoes specially made for him by the blacksmith.

So off went Charlie to ask the blacksmith to make him some shoes. "I want two large shoes," he told him.

"Certainly," said the blacksmith. "Where's your horse?"

"I haven't a horse, they're for me," said Charlie.

"What, no horse? Be off with you, you're making fun of me," shouted the blacksmith.

He looked so fierce that Charlie left in such a hurry that he walked straight into an enormous puddle. Of course he caught *another* cold.

Charlie telephoned for Doctor Dormouse.

"Really, Charlie, this is ridiculous. You *must* stop getting your feet wet," said Doctor Dormouse.

"How can I help it when I haven't any shoes?" sneezed Charlie.

"Shoes? You don't need shoes. I haven't any shoes," said Doctor Dormouse. "I never get my feet wet because I watch where I put them," said Doctor Dormouse.

"Oh," sneezed Charlie. "I never thought of that."

Jurgen the little Danish boy

Jurgen was a little Danish boy who lived in the beautiful city of Copenhagen.

His favourite game was to sit on the grass with his Mother beside the statue of the pretty Copenhagen mermaid and count all the big ships as they sailed into the harbor.

The big ships always made him feel excited. They came from many parts of the world, some of them from places with names difficult to say.

Jurgen said when he grew up he would be a sailor. His daddy was a sailor and when he came home he told Jurgen wonderful stories about the sea.

The story Jurgen loved best was about the Vikings, who sailed from Denmark many years ago to seek new lands.

When Daddy wasn't there to tell it to him, he and Mother would tell it to each other.

The Tale of the Tortoise

Though my age is a hundred and nine,
And my voice is rather a croak.
Trying to be on time,
I'm afraid is a bit of a joke.

If you'd like to help out,
And avoid my being late,
I'm sorry I'll have to shout,
Will you lend me your roller skates!

"They were big fierce looking men with red beards," said Jurgen. "But they were brave to sail all across the sea in wooden boats with only sails to take them along."

"When there wasn't any wind to blow them along they had to row with oars," said Mother.

"Their boats were like this toy one of mine," said Jurgen. "They were called long boats and sometimes, dragon boats. I like that name best, it makes them sound fierce. The Vikings wore helmets with horns sticking out each side, and they carried shields, and spears to fight their enemies. I wish I were a Viking."

"But you can't swim," said Mother. "Vikings must be able to swim."

Jurgen wanted to learn to swim really. It was just that he was afraid to go too far into the water. But Mother said he'd never learn to swim in shallow water. "You must go in far enough to get your feet off the bottom," she said.

Then one day something happened which made him go farther into the water. A little girl lost her beach ball.

She was very upset as it floated away from her. Jurgen watched it float past him and suddenly he decided to rescue it for her.

So he waded in after it and caught it. But then a big wave knocked him off his feet.

He didn't let go of the ball. He clung on tightly and splashed about with his feet. Then Mother came and helped him up.

"I will take the ball and help you swim back to the shore," she said.

And he did!

"Brave boy!" cried the little girl's Mother. And the little girl said, "Please can I come and learn to swim with you?"

Suddenly Jurgen felt he really *wanted* to learn to swim, so he said, "Yes of course you can."

Mother taught them both to swim together. The next time Daddy came home he was very pleased to hear that Jurgen could swim. "Now you can be a real sailor when you grow up," he said.

But Jurgen still wished he could be a Viking.

So Daddy bought him a Viking helmet with horns sticking out each side. "Now you look like a real Viking," he said.

Jurgen felt very proud when he put it on. He wore it when Daddy took him and Mother to look over his ship.

"Hello," said the Captain. "Are you a friendly Viking?"

"Yes," said Jurgen.

"I'm glad," joked the Captain. "I wouldn't like to have to throw you overboard."

"It wouldn't matter if you did. I can swim now," laughed Jurgen.

Katie Fieldmouse's Birthday Party

"What are you giving Katie Fieldmouse for her birthday?" asked Floppity Rabbit.

"Ah, I'm not going to tell anyone," said Bertram Beetle.

"What are you going to give her?" he asked Dolly Dormouse.

"I'm keeping it a big secret," said Dolly Dormouse.

"What are you going to give her," Dolly Dormouse asked Cathie Caterpillar.

"I'm keeping it a secret too," said Cathie.

"What are you giving her, Sally Snail?"

Sally Snail said: "Oh, dear, I don't know what to give her. I'm sure all of you will think of something very splendid and original. I'm so slow at thinking."

"Never mind," said Floppity Rabbit kindly. "I'm sure you'll think of something. But the party's at four o'clock, so you had better hurry."

"You know I can't hurry," said Sally.

"Yes, we know you are rather slow," said Tommy Titmouse, who darted from branch to branch like quicksilver.

"I know," said Sally Snail who had been thinking hard. "I'll give her a little hat."

"Oh, but you've spoiled it by telling us what you are going to give. You should have kept it a secret!" shouted all the friends.

"Just like Sally Snail to be so slow to understand," said Tommy Titmouse.

"Oh," said Sally Snail, "how silly of me!"

"We'll meet at Katie Mouse's house at four o'clock," they all said.

At ten minutes to four by the dandelion clock in the woods there was a little procession of friends winding its way along the hedgerows. The first was Floppity Rabbit. She knocked on the door of Mouse House and Katie's mother let the friends in.

Katie Fieldmouse was so excited when she saw all the presents. The first she opened was from Floppity Rabbit. It was a little tea cozy.

"Thank you," said Katie. "How lovely!"

The next present she opened was from Bertram Beetle. It was *another* tea cozy.

"Thank you, Bertie," said Katie. "That will be nice when the first one is being washed," she said politely.

Next was Dolly Dormouse's present. Do

you know what it was? . . *another* tea cozy.

"Thank you, Dolly," said Katie, just a little more quietly. And she thought of something polite to say. "That will do when . . . when I have special visitors."

The next present was from Cathie Caterpillar. Can you guess what it was? yes, *another* tea cozy.

"Thank you," said Katie. And a little tear crept into the corner of her eye.

"That will match my curtains," she said.

The next present was from Tommy Titmouse. And that was a tea cozy too!

"Thank you," said Katie, with a tiny sob in her voice. "I can use this on Sundays."

At last she came to Sally Snail's present. As Katie started opening it, her little mouth trembled a little. Can you guess what it was? NO, not a tea cozy!

Katie unwrapped the big leaf and inside was the dearest little acorn hat she had ever seen. Sally Snail had put a beautiful blue feather in the hat too.

"Oh, Sally," said Katie. "That is the very nicest present of all!" And she put it on.

"How silly we all were not to tell each other what we were going to give," said Floppity Rabbit. "Sally was the most sensible of us all because she told us what she was going to give."

"What can I do with all my tea cozies?" asked Katie.

"I know," said Sally Snail, who was usually slower than any one else to think of a good idea. "Let's all wear them instead of paper hats at your tea party!"

And that's just what they did!

The lonely house

This is the story of a little house that was miserable. It was sad because it had no one living in it. Every day it looked out of its windows and saw people going in and out of all the other houses in the road, but no one ever came to his door.

"I didn't know that when old Mr. and Mrs. Jones went away they would never come back," he thought sadly. "How happy I would be if children came to live here again. How nice it would be to have them sleeping in my bedrooms and playing with their toys in my living room. I wouldn't mind how much noise they made."

One day, some men came and put up a wooden notice in the front garden of the house just by the gate. It said "FOR SALE."

"Someone is sure to come and buy me soon," said the house, "and then I won't be lonely any more."

That night when the windows of all the other houses were lit up, the little house did not feel at all unhappy.

"MY windows will have lights in them soon," he murmured and went to sleep.

Soon afterwards, a car stopped in the road outside the little house. Out scrambled three children, a dog and three grown ups.

"They are coming to see me, hooray!" chuckled the house.

"Oh, Mother, I'd love to live here!" cried one of the children. "It looks such a friendly house!"

"I certainly like the look of the outside," said her mother. "Come on, let's see what the inside is like."

Down the garden path came the three children, their mother and father and the dog. A key was turned in the lock on the front door and soon the little house was full of chattering. How the house loved it! He felt so happy that somehow his visitors felt it, too.

Jack-In-The-Box

Little pussy found a box,
Which had two tiny locks.
Oh marvellous! she cried.
How I'd love to look inside.

So she opened up the back,
And up sprang Jumping Jack.
Oh dear, cried pussy cat,
You nearly knocked me FLAT.

He didn't even feel miserable after the family had climbed back into their car and driven away. He was sure they would come back and that he was never going to be lonely again.

And he never was. Often after that the children and their mother and father visited him.

They measured his windows for curtains. They measured his floors for carpets. They papered his walls and they painted all his woodwork. Soon he was spick and span all over.

Then, the GREAT DAY arrived—the family moved in.

A huge van arrived outside the little house's gate and soon the rooms were full of men carrying furniture and full of noise and laughter, too, as the children grew more and more excited.

That night, as all the lights in his windows were put out, one by one, the little house thought: "I am the very happiest and luckiest house in the whole village!"

"It feels a happy house, I must say," remarked the father.

"I think we'd be happy here, too," said mother.

The children opened a door into the back garden and ran out.

"Mother! Daddy! There's a swing on an old apple tree!" cried one of them. "It doesn't look as though it's been used for such a long time."

The little house grew happier and happier.

"I'm *sure* they want to come and live in me," he thought.

A Night in the Toy Shop

All day long when boys and girls came in and out of the toy shop the toys sat stiffly up on their shelves.

But at night when the shop was closed they all jumped down and had a jolly time dancing and playing all the games that toys, and little girls and boys liked to play.

One night, Jumbo Elephant said: "Let's all dance!"

And he kicked up his legs and danced a jolly jig in the middle of the shop floor, while the Italian boy doll played a mouth organ.

Soon all the toys were joining him. The Swiss dolls joined hands with the French doll, who joined hands with the Dutch doll and the German doll.

Kangaroo took hold of Teddy Bear, who took hold of Panda who took hold of Susan with the golden ear-rings.

Round and round they whirled while Puffin, penguin and the yellow duck danced a little dance all by themselves.

The fairy doll waved her magic wand and all the balloons came floating down from the stick they'd been tied to in the corner.

Rabbit wound up the clockwork mouse and he scuttled in and out among the dancers.

Soon everyone was dancing—everyone excepting monkey. And he as usual was getting up to mischief.

He had found a bag of marbles and was

sitting in a corner watching the dancers with an artful look in his eye.

Suddenly he tipped up the bag and let all the marbles roll across the floor.

"All fall down," he chuckled as the dancers began tripping over them.

Down they fell one after another and naughty monkey laughed louder and louder.

But he didn't laugh for long. Because guardsman doll and policeman doll picked themselves up and came quickly across to him and seized him by his ears.

"Say you're sorry this minute or we'll put you up on the dusty shelf," said policeman doll.

Monkey quickly said he was sorry. He didn't want to be put up on the dusty shelf which was the highest shelf in the shop and close to the ceiling.

Nobody would see him up there and it was unlikely he'd be brought down again until the shopkeeper had a sale. Then he'd be brought down and marked 'half price.'

Monkey didn't fancy that at all.

So he said he was very sorry and he'd pick up all the marbles.

Which he did. But he kept one.

"Look," said Rabbit. "The sun is rising, it will soon be time to open the shop."

"Goodness, we must climb back on our shelves," cried Jumbo Elephant.

So all the toys and all the dolls climbed back up on to their shelves. And when the shopkeeper came and opened the door there they were sitting up stiff and straight as though they'd never stirred all night.

But as the shopkeeper walked towards his counter a marble rolled across the floor.

He didn't fall over it though. He stopped and picked it up. "I wonder where that came from," he said. And he slipped it in his pocket.

Monkey grinned. He knew where it had come from. He had thrown it. It just seemed he couldn't help being a naughty monkey. Maybe he didn't really believe the toys would ever put him up on that dusty shelf.

Cathie Postman

Every morning Cathie went down the garden path on her tricycle and waited at the garden gate for the postman. She knew which way he would come because he always came exactly the same way every morning. He never changed.

At Number Seven the gate squeaked when the postman went in and again when he came out. At Number Nine the dog barked and rushed out at the postman. He often passed old Mrs. Jones' door at Number Eleven, because she didn't get letters every day. At Number Thirteen, the cat stood up and arched its back to welcome the postman.

After that it was Cathie's house—Number Fifteen.

"Good morning," said the postman.

"Good morning," said Cathie.

"Four letters for your house today," he said. "I guess you've got a visitor staying with you, haven't you?"

"Yes, it's my auntie. How did you guess?" asked Cathie.

"Because there's a letter for a Mrs. Baker at your house."

"That's my auntie's name," said Cathie.

And she cycled ting-a-ling up the garden path, just to let Mother know that she was coming in to breakfast.

"There's a letter for Auntie," said Cathie. "May I take it up to her?"

"We'll put it on her breakfast tray," said Mother.

Auntie *was* pleased with the letter. "I've

Kites fly
Up in the sky.
When the wind blows
Away it goes.
So hold the string tight
With all your might.
Or you will lose
Your colorful kite.

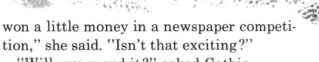

won a little money in a newspaper competition," she said. "Isn't that exciting?"

"Will you spend it?" asked Cathie.

"Oh, I will put it in the bank," said Auntie. "I don't spend every bit of money as I get it, that would be silly, because I don't win competitions every day."

Auntie went off to the shops all by herself and came back at lunch time.

She had a package.

"Did you go to the Bank?" asked Cathie.

"Yes," said Auntie, "but I didn't put all the money in the Bank. I bought a little something for the postman who brought my lucky letter this morning."

"Oh, what is it?" asked Cathie.

"You may open it and see if you think the postman will like it," said Auntie.

Cathie loved opening packages, even if they weren't for her. Inside was a postman's hat and a postman's jacket and trousers and a postman's bag.

"Oh, they are lovely," said Cathie. "But they are *much* too small for him. He's a very big postman, you know."

"Never mind," said Auntie, "try them on."

Cathie tried them on and they fitted her.

"You may have them," said Auntie.

"Oh, Auntie, thank you," said Cathie. "What will you get for the postman instead?"

"But you *are* the postman, aren't you?" said Auntie. "Every morning while I've been staying with you, I've been watching

you from my bedroom window. I've seen you ride down to the gate and take the letters and bring them indoors. I heard you go ting-a-ling along the garden path. So I thought you were the postman."

"Yes, I am," said Cathie.

And the next day she put on her postman's uniform and went on her tricycle to the gate.

The postman was surprised when he saw her in uniform.

"My, you have become a real postman," he said. "Next Christmas when I'm really busy, you will have to come and help me."

Cathie took the letters and went ting-a-ling back to the kitchen door, and she wore the uniform every day after that.

The Race

My name is Queen Mab and I live in a fine pigeon loft with lots of other racing pigeons. We belong to Mr. Mick and we think he is the best pigeon fancier in the whole world. No matter where we may be, we do our best to fly home to him as quickly as possible, for no one else could care for us as he does.

Our loft has every comfort and Mr Mick's dog sleeps in a kennel by our house.

The other day, I was sitting on a perch in the garden, when Mr Mick came out. I flew on to his shoulder.

"Hello," he said, "and how is my champion this morning? Are you going to win the big race all the way home from France?"

"I'll do my best," I cooed.

The next morning, Mr. Mick took me along to his Pigeon Racing Club. He held me gently while another man wrote down the number that is stamped on the little metal ring I wear on my leg.

"Now we'll put your race ring on," said the man, "then into the basket you'll go!"

There were several other pigeons I knew in the travelling basket. Soon all the other pigeons who were racing from France with us were safely in their baskets and we were loaded onto a van.

"We're off!" cried the van driver. "We shall soon be on the Channel Ferry!"

"Good-by! Good luck!" Mr Mick called.

I get very sleepy on these long journeys and I would want all my strength for the flight home. So I slept most of the time as we drove across France.

I woke up with a start when the pigeon next to me gave me a friendly peck.

"Wake up!" he said, "I think we've arrived."

"I wonder where we are?" I said to my friend.

"I heard a man say we were being set free in the mountains between France and Spain," he replied.

"What a long way from home," I thought. "I wish they'd hurry up!"

It wasn't long before each of our basket doors were opened and we all flew out. There were hundreds and hundreds of us and I expect we looked just like a gray cloud. How good it was to be free and to have the whole blue sky to ourselves. But already I was thinking of Mr. Mick and Rusty and our pigeon loft.

"Cheerio!" I called to my friend, "I'm off!"

of time until a cheeky starling flew by.

"Going to see the sights of Paris?" he squawked. "There are some good perches on the Eiffel Tower."

"No, I'm *not*," I said crossly, "I'm going home." But I looked down, all the same, and there below me was the tallest tower I've ever seen, and the city spread around it looked very inviting. But I flew on, and when I saw the busy port with the big ships and the bustling little tugs, I knew I was not far from home.

The sun was setting as I flew over Mr. Mick's bungalow and on to the landing

On through the snow-capped mountains I flew and as the sun faded, I saw a great black cloud coming up all round me. Then there was a loud bang and a flash of light across the sky and down came the rain. I was blown all over the place, I can tell you.

As I left the mountains the storm died away and when daylight came I saw I was flying over green wooded country, silvery rivers and old castles. Then I lost count

board of our loft. And there was Mr. Mick and Rusty, waiting for me.

"There's Queen Mab! There's my champion!" he shouted.

How happy I was to be safely home. I was so tired that I fell asleep right away.

That was a week ago. Mr Mick has just come out into the garden.

"You've won! You've won!" he shouted. "You really are a champion, Queen Mab!"

The Taxi drive

Bill, the London taxi, woke up one morning feeling ill and grumpy.

"I don't think I shall go out today," he thought, "my inside does not feel at all right." At that moment Bill's driver, Tom, came into the garage.

"Good morning, Bill," he said, "time to go to work." He climbed into the driving seat and switched on the taxi's engine. Bill coughed, spluttered and hiccupped into silence.

"Poor old fellow," muttered Tom, "I wonder what's wrong; I must look under your hood."

For several minutes Tom worked away at

Bill's engine and gradually the taxi began to feel very much better. "Now let's try again," said Tom and this time when he switched on, Bill's engine purred smoothly.

"I think I *will* go out after all," the taxi murmured.

Soon, in bright sunshine, Bill and Tom were on their way.

"What a lovely day, I *am* glad I came out," thought Bill, and in no time at all Tom was driving through the gates of Waterloo Station to the Main Line Entrance. This is where they started work each day.

"My goodness, what a lot of customers

there are this morning," cried Tom. "Hold on, Bill, let's stop at the top of the line!"

"Here's our taxi, mother, it's our turn, now!" cried a little boy, as Bill drew up.

"So it is, Charles," replied his mother. "Let's ask the taxi driver if he can help us." She smiled at Tom.

"We've just arrived in London and have two hours to wait for our next train. My son has never been to London before, could you take us to see some of the sights, please?"

"Certainly, madam," replied Tom.

"Hooray!" shouted Charles.

"Hooray!" thought Bill. "I *am* glad my

engine feels better—what fun it will be."

And it *was* the greatest fun for Charles and his mother and for Tom and Bill, too. They admired the Thames from Westminster Bridge and waved to the boats beneath. They heard Big Ben strike the hour and were just in time to see the changing of the guard at Buckingham Palace.

Charles nearly fell out of Bill's window with excitement when he saw the soldiers in their scarlet jackets and tall, black, fur hats marching smartly by.

They gazed up at Nelson's Column in Trafalgar Square; laughed at the fountains sparkling in the sun and at the hundreds of pigeons strutting about and tamely feeding out of people's hands.

Tom said that if Bill was very clever in dodging the traffic they would just have time to drive past St. Paul's Cathedral and into the City to the Tower of London.

"I'll be as quick as I can," promised Bill, and very soon they were admiring the great dome of St. Paul's. Then off they whisked through the narrow City streets to the Tower of London. The White Tower looked grand against the blue sky and Tom pointed out the famous ravens of the Tower perched on the battlements.

"Do you know," said Tom, "there is a story which says that if those great, black birds ever leave the Tower of London, something terrible will happen but they have

never, ever flown away. Well, time to go back to Waterloo station."

With five minutes to spare, Bill pulled up at the Main Line Entrance again. Charles' face was flushed with enjoyment as he clambered out.

"Thank you very much," he said, "that was wonderful. I wish I could have spent all day with you and your taxi."

"So do I," said Tom.

"So do I," said Bill to himself as they watched Charles and his mother disappear into the station.

Sammy Squirrel's happy Christmas

Sammy Squirrel was busy collecting nuts to store away for the winter. "When winter comes there will be no nuts left on the trees," he told Mr. Pixie, who was looking for wood for his fire.

"I thought you slept all through the winter, Sammy," said Mr. Pixie.

"Lots of people think that. But I don't," said Sammy. "I sleep quite a lot, but on sunny days, when the weather is a little bit warmer I wake up. Then I feel hungry. So I take a few nuts from my store and have a nice meal."

"I see," said Mr. Pixie. "Well, good-by. I hope you'll find a lovely lot of nuts for your store."

Sammy did. When Mr. Pixie passed by with his wheelbarrow on the way home Sammy had a huge pile of nuts.

"You have found a lot of nuts. You must feel pleased, Sammy," said Mr. Pixie.

Sammy wasn't pleased. He was worried. Because while he had been busy collecting his nuts all the other squirrels had filled the best storing places. "There's nowhere left for mine," he cried.

Mr. Pixie put down his wheelbarrow. He hadn't been lucky in finding much wood because all the other pixies had gathered it before him.

"I have a place to store my wood, but not much wood to store in it," he said.

Then he cried "Sammy, I've had an idea. Why don't you store your nuts in my woodshed? You could sleep in the box on the shelf above. Nobody would disturb you because nobody goes in there but me. I would always creep in very quietly."

Sammy thought it a wonderful idea. So together they loaded the nuts on to Mr. Pixie's wheelbarrow and off they went.

When they reached his woodshed, they put the wood in one corner and the nuts in the other, and Sammy climbed up to the box on the shelf, into which Mr. Pixie kindly put leaves and grass to make him a comfortable bed.

He soon went off to sleep, and whenever Mr. Pixie came into the shed for some wood he crept in quietly so as not to wake him.

Then one day Mr. Pixie came for some wood and found there was none left. He was upset. "It's Christmas Day, and I cannot have

a fire to sit by and have my dinner," he cried.

He had not realized he'd spoken aloud.

But Sammy happened to be awake and he heard him. "Look in my corner, you will find plenty of wood for your fire," he said.

There was indeed. Every time Sammy had taken a feed of nuts he'd dropped the nut-shells on the floor. "You can burn them on your fire," said Sammy.

Mr. Pixie was grateful. He filled a basket with the shells and together with a few twigs and fir cones he happened to find he soon made a beautiful fire.

"Come and have Christmas dinner with me," he called to Sammy.

Sammy was pleased. He'd never been to Christmas dinner with anyone before. He brought some of his nuts, and Mr. Pixie gave him some cherries from a jar.

"I've heard squirrels like cherries," he smiled.

What a happy day they had together. "We must do this again next year," laughed Mr. Pixie.

"I would like that," smiled Sammy.

Ballet shoes
Are soft and slippery,
Made to point the toe
So prettily.

Football boots
Are hard and rough,
Made to play a game
That's tough!

Clucky, the Hen who liked to wander

Clucky the hen liked to wander. Anywhere, everywhere, she'd go. She didn't care where she went as long as it wasn't into her nest box in the hen house to lay eggs.

"Cluck," she'd say to the other hens. "I'm not wasting my time laying eggs."

"You'll be sorry," the other hens clucked after her one day, when she squeezed through a hole in the hedge and ran off into the wood. "Take care."

Clucky thought they said, "Take Hare."

"Perhaps, I will," she said to herself. "He would be company for me and he wouldn't want to talk about laying eggs all day long. I'll go and look for him."

She didn't find Hare, but she met Fox.

"You're a nice looking hen," said Fox.

"Do you really think so?" asked Clucky.

"Yes," said Fox, coming a bit nearer. "Nice enough to eat."

"Oh no," said Clucky hastily. "I'm not all that nice."

"Well, I like you," said Fox. "Where are you going?"

"I'm off to find Hare," said Clucky.

"I'd like to find Hare. I'll come with you," said Fox. "Have you any idea which hole he might live in?"

"Hares don't live in holes. You're thinking of rabbits. Hares live in the long grass," said Clucky.

"Now that's interesting," said Fox, with

The Piggy Bank

What did my little piggy take?
I think he has a tummy ache.
He clanks about the house all day,
And even tried to run away.
He must have eaten too much money,
No wonder he is feeling funny!

an artful gleam in his eye. "There's some long grass over there. Let's go and see if Hare is anywhere about."

Hare was dozing in the long grass. But when he heard Clucky clucking away he peeped out and saw Fox. And he took a big leap and bounded away through the wood.

"Now there's only you and me," cried Fox grinning. He opened his mouth wide and showed all his big teeth.

Clucky was scared. "It's not true," she cried. "There are lots of rabbits in the wood."

"But *they* are safely down their holes," said Fox.

"There are some squirrels," said Clucky.

"*They* are all safely up in the trees," said Fox.

Clucky was wishing she was safely back in her nest box in the hen house.

She quickly said, "There's Farmer's dog."

"Where?" cried Fox, spinning round.

"Over there," cried Clucky as she dashed away through the wood.

Fox rushed after her. She managed to scramble through the hedge just as he snapped his jaws, and missed her.

What a clucking she made! Luckily Farmer's dog *was* on the other side of the hedge—looking for her. Farmer had taught him to search the hedge for stray hens, so he barked loudly as she scrambled through, to let Farmer know he'd found her.

He barked louder still when he saw Fox peering through the hedge at him.

Fox disappeared down the nearest foxhole he could find.

"Ah, a stray hen," cried Farmer when he saw Clucky. "Good dog, what should we do without you?"

Clucky stayed in her nest box in the hen house for the rest of the day. When at last she came out she'd laid three eggs.

"Aren't you going to wander?" the other hens asked her.

"I've seen all that I want to see on the other side of the hedge," said Clucky.

Petros, Pietro, Pierre, Pedro, Pieter, Pyotr

*(spell it how you will—in English they all mean—*PETER.)

Pietro is Italian. He lives in the beautiful city of Venice.

His daddy is a gondolier. Sometimes he lets Pietro come with him when he takes visitors for a ride in his gondola.

Pietro likes this because his daddy sings as they punt along the canals. There are lots of canals in Venice and many bridges over them. Pietro lives near one of the best known bridges called the Bridge of Sighs.

Pierre is a little French boy. His daddy owns a vineyard and in September when the grapes are ripe they are picked and loaded into a cart drawn by oxen.

Everybody is very happy when the grapes have all been picked because then they can have a holiday. They all dress up in their best clothes and sing and dance through the village streets and taste the wine made from the grapes.

Pieter lives in Holland near a pretty Dutch windmill. His daddy grows tulips, red, white and yellow. And lovely blue hyacinths and golden daffodils.

In the spring Pieter and his mother have a ride in daddy's barge along the canal which runs through his fields.

They sit among the flowers that daddy has picked to sell at the market.

English Peter has a cuckoo clock. He loves all clocks. He lives in London near "Big Ben" which is a very famous clock.

His daddy is a taxi driver but Peter likes to ride on top of the big red double decker buses.

Sometimes he visits the Tower of London with his mother and sees the "Beefeaters" in their scarlet uniforms.

Petros is a little Greek boy. He lives in the port of Piraeus near Athens. His daddy is captain of a steamer.

Petros spends most of his day on the wharf looking at the gaily painted boats moored in the harbor.

Sometimes he sits and listens to the exciting stories told by his fishermen friends while they mend their nets.

In the spring his daddy takes him on his steamer across to the Island of Poros to see the beautiful lemon trees in bloom.

Petros will be a sailor when he grows up.

Pedro is Portuguese and lives on the island of Madeira.

His daddy has a bullock cart and takes holiday makers for rides in it.

Pedro's family do not have much money but they are happy to live on this sunny island which has many brightly colored flowers growing everywhere, and plenty of banana plantations.

Pedro's mother is a "flower lady" and sells her flowers from a big basket which she carries on her head. She wears a gay red dress and white boots and looks very smart.

Peter lives in Germany, in the Black Forest. His daddy is a wood carver and makes weather houses and cuckoo clocks and lots of toys.

Sometimes Peter helps him in his workshop.

Some of the toys are sent to England where little English Peter sees them in the toy shops.

And so we come to *Pyotr* who lives far away in Russia.

His daddy is a manager on a big farm and Pyotr does not often visit the town.

In winter when the snow is very deep Pyotr has to wrap up in lots of warm clothes, and if the family need to travel very far they ride in a "Troika" which is a kind of sleigh, drawn by three horses.

Peter Penguin

Peter Penguin stood on the snow covered ice and watched the birds circling above his head. And he flapped his stiff little flippers and wondered why he couldn't fly with them.

But he couldn't and it made him cross.

When the other birds flew off towards the sea he tried to follow them. But with his short little legs all Peter could do was waddle and hop—and hop and waddle, until at last he fell flop on his tummy.

"I will get to the sea, I will," he cried.

So Peter wriggled and slid and pushed and wriggled until at last he did get there—all the way on his tummy.

There were many penguins in the sea. "Come and join us," they cried.

Peter penguin hurried into the water. He found he could swim very well with his firm little flippers. Soon he was speeding through the water.

He soon made lots of friends and most of them were Emperor penguins like himself.

"There are other kinds of penguins," said another penguin called Patty. "There are

King penguins, and Adelie penguins and lots of other kinds, but they don't live near here."

"Oh, I see," said Peter penguin.

Each day as he grew bigger and stronger Peter showed Patty how he could flip through the water faster than ever before.

Then one day Patty penguin said she'd like to go ashore and lay an egg, like so many of the other lady penguins seemed to be doing.

"I will come with you and help you make a nest," said Peter penguin.

So they both waddled and hopped and slid across the ice to find somewhere to make a nest.

But they couldn't find a cozy place anywhere. They couldn't even find anything with which to make a nest.

At last Patty penguin grew tired of looking. "I shall lay my egg right here," she cried.

She did! She laid it right on Peter penguins feet. "Don't drop it," she told him. "Keep it warm while I go back to the sea to get something to eat."

But she took a long time getting something to eat. And it was cold standing there with the egg between his toes.

Peter penguin looked around him. Standing near him were lots of other penguins holding eggs between their feet.

"Are you cold?" he asked them.

They all said they were.

"Then let us hop together and keep ourselves and our eggs warm," said Peter penguin.

Holding their eggs carefully the penguins hopped in closer together. And there they stayed until at long last their eggs were hatched and out came the little penguin chicks.

Just as the father penguins were wondering what to do with their little chicks, back came the mother penguins looking sleek and fat and full of fish.

"Sorry we've been so long. Your turn now," they called as they hurried up.

So they took care of the chicks while the father penguins slid off down to the sea to find some food.

And when they'd had enough to eat they came back to help the mother penguins take care of the young penguins.

Soon the young penguins were big enough to take care of themselves. So what did they do? One day they all waddled and hopped— and hopped and slid on their tummies all the way down to the sea—just like their parents.

Elizabeth's magic Rocking Horse

Elizabeth had a magic rocking horse. By sitting on its back and rocking it to and fro, she could make it change into any kind of horse she wished—such as a sea horse or a cloud horse. Then they would go on wonderful adventures down through the sea or up among the clouds.

One morning she said, "I think I'll change you into a sea horse today."

So she climbed up on to the magic rocking-horse and started to rock him to and fro. "To and fro, down in the sea we go," she sang as she rocked.

And soon they were sinking through the waves, right to the sandy bottom of the sea.

"Hello," called a mermaid. "Come and play with me."

Elizabeth tied her horse to an old anchor, with a long piece of seaweed and went off to play with the mermaid.

As they passed the shell of a hermit crab the mermaid called, "Coming out to play?"

But the hermit crab didn't answer.

"He's so shy, he never speaks to anyone," said the mermaid. "So of course he hasn't any friends. How can you make friends if you never speak to anyone at all?"

Elizabeth didn't have time to answer because some fish called skates came along just then. They weren't shy.

"Coming skating with us?" they cried. "We're just off to find a nice big iceberg."

"Silly things, they won't find one round here," laughed the mermaid. "The water's much too warm. Oh, here comes my dog," she said.

"How can you have a dog down here in the sea," cried Elizabeth with surprise.

Then she saw it was a dogfish.

"You have dog animals on land, and we have dogfish in the sea," laughed the mermaid.

But suddenly she looked worried. Her pearl necklace had come undone. "The clasp needs tightening" she said. "Let's find a lobster to do it for me."

They soon found a lobster who pinched the clasp tighter for her. "That's better," smiled the mermaid. "I mustn't lose these pearls because they're real. Some oyster friends of mine made them specially for me. It took them a very long time."

"I'm glad then that you haven't lost it," said Elizabeth politely.

Then she said, "I ought to be going home."

"Would you like some periwinkles to take home with you?" asked the mermaid.

"Yes, please, I like periwinkles," said Elizabeth.

She was surprised when the mermaid gave her a handful of winkles. "These are not flowers," she cried. "Periwinkles are blue flowers."

"They are also sea snails," said the mermaid. "You call them winkles, which is only short for periwinkle."

Elizabeth thanked her for the periwinkles and went to untie her sea horse.

Then up, up through the waves they rose. "Oh dear," she cried as they came up out of the sea. "I've dropped my winkles."

"Stop nodding your head," she cried to the sea horse, as she tried to peer down into the water to look for them.

But it was Elizabeth who was nodding her head for she had fallen asleep on her magic rocking horse.

"We'll have another adventure tomorrow," she told him, climbing down. "We've found out lots of new things today, haven't we."

New dungarees for Timothy

Timothy's Mother bought him a lovely new pair of dungarees. They went to the shops together to choose them. Timothy chose a red pair, and he liked them so much that, when he tried them on in the shop, he didn't want to take them off again.

"Would you like to keep them on to go home in?" asked the saleslady.

"Yes, please," said Timothy. And the lady let him walk out of the shop wearing his lovely new dungarees.

"They are to wear over your other things to keep your clothes clean while you play in the garden," explained Mother.

When they got home, Timothy went straight out in the garden. He was soon having fun in his sandpit and completely forgot he was wearing his new dungarees until he heard Jane from next door. She was peeping over the fence.

"Oh, Timothy, you've got new trousers on," said Jane. "Aren't they lovely?"

Timothy ran over to Jane.

"I've got something new too," said Jane. "If you peep over the fence you will see it."

Timothy went to his special place in the fence where he always climbed up, and looked over into Jane's garden.

There on Jane's lawn was a lovely yellow scooter.

"Oh, Jane, you are lucky," said Timothy. "May I ride it?"

"Yes," said Jane. "Ask your Mother if you can come this afternoon."

Timothy jumped down very quickly, but as he jumped, he caught his new dungarees on a splinter of wood—and tore them.

One minute he was excited about Jane's scooter and the next minute he was crying about his new dungarees. What would Mother say? He ran into the kitchen.

"Mother, look what I've done to my new dungarees!"

"Oh, dear," said Mother. "That *is* a big tear!" Then Mother was very quiet for a minute.

"Are you cross?" asked Timothy.

"No, I'm not *very* cross," said Mother. "That's what dungarees are for, to save your other clothes. But I'm thinking of a way to mend them so that no one will know. Now I've thought of a way."

Little Gosling

Mrs. Goosey out one day,
Lost a gosling on the way.
O dear, O dear, Mrs. Goosey cried,
Where has that gosling gone to hide?

So in the bushes and by the stream,
Mrs. Goosey looked for him.
But little gosling was having fun,
Nibbling grass in the summer sun.

The sun went behind a big, black cloud,
And little gosling called out loud,
It wasn't a good idea to roam,
Before it rains, I will go straight home.

Timothy took them off.

"Aren't you really and truly cross?" asked Timothy.

"No," said Mother. "Even big grown-up men tear their dungarees when they are very busy."

Timothy watched Mother go to her sewing basket. She brought out a piece of green material and a piece of yellow material.

"Now, what picture would you like me to patch this big tear with?" she asked.

Timothy thought for a long time, then he said: "An airplane."

So Mother cut out the yellow material for the body of the airplane and then she cut out the green material for the wings and the tail. Then she sewed the picture over the tear and no one could see that there had been a tear at all!

And that afternoon, when Timothy went round to Jane's house to have a ride on her scooter, Jane said: "I didn't notice that lovely airplane on your dungarees this morning!"

And Timothy didn't tell her about the tear—that was a big secret between him and his Mother, wasn't it?

Robbie and the Fox

Robbie, Mother and Daddy had moved from the big town where they'd always lived, and gone to live in the country.

They'd only been there a week and Robbie was missing all the things he'd liked in the big town. He missed the shops and street lamps and all the people. He didn't think he liked the country very much.

It was so quiet where they lived now. Just their cottage and a farm down the lane.

"You'll make some friends when we've been here a bit longer," said Mother. "The country is an interesting place to live in really."

She showed Robbie a book with pictures of country animals in it. There was a hedgehog, some field mice and a fox. Robbie said the fox looked a bit like a dog, with a big bushy tail. He said he'd like to see the fox.

"You may have to wait a long time," said Daddy. "The fox only comes out when it's getting dark, and it doesn't let people see it very often."

"Why not?" asked Robbie.

"Because people, especially farmers, don't like foxes. Foxes are naughty and try to steal chickens," said Daddy.

"Where do the foxes live?" asked Robbie.

Daddy pointed across the garden. "They live up there in that little wood on the side of the hill," he said. "They live in holes, like the rabbits."

One afternoon Mother took Robbie up the hill to the wood to pick primroses and violets. And they saw some foxes' holes. The holes were half hidden away under some bramble bushes so they were lucky to find them.

But they didn't see a fox.

Soon it was time to go home because the sun was setting and by the time they reached their lane it had set behind the hill, and made the clouds pink and golden. Then all too soon it started to grow dark.

"We must hurry now," Mother told Robbie.

"I can't. I'm tired," said Robbie.

So they had to walk slowly home along the lane.

him. Daddy thought perhaps they ought to telephone the farmer to let him know a fox was around his chicken houses.

The farmer thanked Daddy and the next morning he came with his children to invite Robbie and his parents to see his farm.

Robbie soon made friends with the farmer's children, and he felt very proud when they said they'd lived there all their lives and never seen a fox. He'd only lived there one week and already seen one.

"I like living in the country," he said suddenly.

Mother smiled. "Somehow I thought you would—when you grew used to it," she said.

"We're nearly there," said Mother at last. "Just one corner to turn."

As they turned the corner of the lane they noticed something in the middle of the road.

They stopped and stared. "Oh," whispered Mummy. "I do believe it's a fox."

Robbie felt so excited. He wanted to get near enough to have a good look at it.

The fox didn't seem to know they were behind him. He started to move slowly along the lane, while Mother and Robbie crept behind him.

Every now and then he stopped and looked around him, and then they stopped too, until he moved on.

But as they neared the gate of the farm the fox swiftly disappeared through a hole in the hedge.

Robbie rushed indoors to tell Daddy about

Mickey Monkey's Tricks

Micky the monkey was always in trouble, and no wonder, because he was always up to his naughty monkey tricks.

He lived on a farm and all the other animals were always getting cross with him because he did such naughty things.

One day Mick was in the big feeding shed where Mr. Giles the farmer was busy putting out all the food for the animals.

"Now," said Mr Giles to his wife. "Today I have to go out and will not be back for feeding time. Will you feed the animals for me? Everything's ready so that you will not have anything to do except to give the right food to the right animals at five o'clock."

Micky heard this and thought he would like to feed the animals. He wanted to help.

So, when it was nearly five o'clock, he put the hands of the clock *back* so that Mrs.

Giles thought it was only *four* o'clock. Then Micky went to the feeding shed.

He gave a big bowl of bones to the cow. She didn't like that at all.

He gave a bowl of fish to the horse. He didn't like that at all.

He gave a bowl of corn to the dog. He didn't like that at all.

He gave a bunch of bananas to the chickens. They didn't like that at all.

He gave a bowl of cow-cake to the cat. She didn't like that at all.

At six o'clock when Mrs. Giles came out to feed the animals because she thought it

was *five* o'clock, she heard a dreadful noise in the farmyard.

The cow was mooing because she didn't like the dog's food. The horse was neighing because he didn't like the cat's food. The dog was barking because he didn't like the chicken's food. The cat was mewing because she didn't like the cow's food. And the chickens were clucking because they didn't like the bananas.

When Mrs. Giles saw the bananas, which were really the monkey's food, she knew what had happened. So she smiled to herself and found the only food that was left—a big bundle of hay, which was really the horse's food—and gave it to Micky. Poor Micky didn't like that either, so he began to cry.

"Serves you right for muddling up all the food," said Mrs. Giles.

Poor Micky didn't have any supper that night and he never played that trick again. But he still plays other naughty tricks. He can't really help it because all monkeys get up to monkey tricks, don't they?

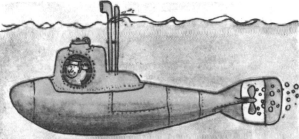

Down beneath the ocean green,
Lay a little submarine,
The captain, who was rather tubby,
Looked out and found it rather muddy.

'We'll stick,' he cried, 'Into the mud,
Because we sank with such a thud.
To rise again, I must be thinner,
I'll have to go without my dinner!'

Haymaking Time

Uncle Jeremy's combine harvester went round and round the hayfield. Philip stood high on the bank and watched it gobble up the long grass, magically parcel it and then toss it like huge hay bricks behind it.

Uncle Jeremy had started cutting from the outside edge of the field and then he drove the machine round and round in smaller and smaller circles towards the middle. Philip wondered what would happen when the combine harvester reached the *very* middle. But the field was very big and Uncle Jeremy didn't finish it before lunch.

At last Uncle Jeremy stopped the machine, jumped down and walked across to Philip.

"Let's have our sandwiches" he shouted.

Philip ran to where the two sacks of sandwiches lay in the shade under the tree. Philip had a little sack all to himself and he

felt like a grown-up farmer as he took out his sandwiches and flask of cool drink.

"After lunch," said Uncle Jeremy, "I will finish cutting this field and you will see lots of rabbits running out as the patch of grass in the middle gets smaller and smaller. Will you count them for me?"

"Yes," said Philip. Uncle Jeremy finished his sandwiches and lay back on the grass with his hat over his eyes and went to sleep. But he soon jumped up and said: "Back to work!"

Philip watched impatiently for the first rabbit to run out of the grass. There it went, helter-skelter across the field and into the hedgerow.

Then another, and another . . . soon there were more rabbits than Philip could count. One came darting out and went zig-zagging across the field, leaping as it went. It had very long ears and was *much* bigger than the other rabbits.

Uncle Jeremy had seen it too. He stopped the engine and told Philip that it was a hare—not a rabbit.

Philip wondered how Uncle Jeremy would cut the very last piece of grass—it stood up like a tuft of newly washed hair.

But Uncle Jeremy stopped the machine again and came across to Philip. "Would you like to pretend to be a rabbit and hide in that tiny island of grass just before I cut it?"

"Oh, yes!" said Philip. He ran across and started to crawl into the island of grass. But suddenly he stopped.

There just in front of him was a tiny baby rabbit crouched down and far too frightened to race out across the open field.

"May I keep him for a pet?" he asked Uncle Jeremy.

"Well, no," said Uncle Jeremy. "That would be unkind. You see how frightened he is already. And it's a leveret, too—that's a baby hare. Look at its extra long back legs for leaping with! He would be so unhappy in a rabbit hutch."

Philip was disappointed, but he took the leveret to the hedge and placed him gently in the long grass. The leveret did not move. He went on crouching until Philip went away.

At last the field was finished, the last tuft of grass had been cut and they were ready for home. Philip took one quick look in the hedge. The leveret had gone.

"You are a very kind boy," said Uncle Jeremy. "That little leveret will always remember you for letting him live a lovely wild life with all his friends."

Billy's Birthday Adventure

Billy was in bed with a cold. On his birthday too. It was a shame. He'd been looking forward to his special birthday drive in the car with Mother and the birthday tea afterwards.

"Never mind," said Mother. "We can have the birthday tea up here in the bedroom, and we can have a 'pretend' birthday drive."

Mother hurried to get all her jobs in the house finished quickly.

"Now," she said when at last she was ready. "Where shall we go?"

"I'll ask my birthday Panda," said Billy.

"Panda says he'd like to go and see some more pandas," said Billy after he'd whispered in Panda's ear.

"All right, we'll pretend to go to the Zoo," said Mother.

"Oh no, he says he wants to go where the real pandas live," said Billy.

"Goodness, that would be China," said Mother. "It's a long way; we couldn't go by car."

"We'll go in my toy airplane," said Billy.

"All right then. Close your eyes and let's start pretending now," said Mother.

Billy closed his eyes. "We're off," he said. "We're flying very high. Now we're looking down through the clouds and I can see China."

"I can see some trees, I think it's a big forest," said Mother.

"Panda says it's where his family lives. We'd better land now," said Billy.

"Bring the plane down carefully," said Mother. "We have to land on the side of this big mountain and it's all covered with snow."

"We're down," cried Billy. "Out you get, Panda. Oh dear," he added, "Panda's run away."

"I wonder where he's gone," said Mother. "I can't see anything but snow around here, except that bit of black tree-stump over there."

"Well I never, would you believe it," she laughed. "It's not a tree-stump at all, it's Panda. He's just turned round and looked at me. I really thought he was a tree-stump in the snow."

"I expect that's why he's colored black and white," said Billy. "So that he can't be seen in the snow. Then he'd be safe from people who came to hunt him, because they would think he was just a piece of old tree and pass by."

"Yes, how clever of you, Billy. I'm sure you're right," said Mother." Well, shall we go across to the forest now?"

"I will walk in front with Panda, and if he sees anyone we don't like he can frighten them away for us," said Billy.

"Good," said Mother. "I'll follow close behind. Can you see anything exciting yet?"

"Ooh, yes, I can see lots of Pandas," cried Billy. "I think they're having their tea."

"They would be eating bamboo shoots then," said Mother. "That's what Pandas eat in their own country. There'd be nothing else for them in this forest."

"I don't want bamboo-shoots for my birthday tea," said Billy. "I think we'll go home and have my birthday cake now."

It was lucky they decided to do this, because just then Daddy came home.

"We've been to China for my birthday," said Billy.

"Did you take Bamboo-Eater with you?" asked Daddy, picking up Panda.

"Why did you call him that?" asked Billy.

"Because that's his name. Panda means Bamboo-Eater," explained Daddy.

When Billy was better he went to the Zoo to see the real Panda. "Hello, Bamboo-Eater," he cried. "That's what Panda really means," he told the surprised keeper.

I am a little penguin,
And would you like to know?
That I live at the South Pole,
And it is white with snow.

And though I have a pair of wings,
And though I really try,
When I jump into the air,
I cannot really fly.

Oliver Octopus takes a Job

Oliver Octopus was an adventurous young octopus. He swam further from home than any of his brothers. He wanted to go and see what life was like ashore. So he let the tide take him, and he floated lazily on a big wave which swooshed him on to the beach.

"This is fun," said Oliver.

He climbed up the beach. The first thing he saw was a beach cafe. Lots of people were waiting to be served at the tables under the big umbrellas outside. They were getting very impatient as there did not seem to be a waiter anywhere.

Suddenly a man came hurrying out of the cafe. He was Mr. Chips, the manager.

"Oh dear," he was saying to himself. "What am I going to do? All these people are waiting for lunch and my waiter has not turned up yet."

"Can I help you?" asked Oliver.

"Well," said Mr. Chips, who was very surprised to see an octopus. "I have never had an octopus working for me before. But you have lots of arms. I could do with an extra pair of hands."

"I have *eight* arms," said Oliver, proudly. "I'm walking on two of them, so that leaves six for carrying things."

"How splendid," said Mr. Chips. "Come to the kitchen and I'll show you what to do."

The chef showed Oliver a sideboard full of plates of food waiting to be carried to the people outside.

"Do you think you could carry a few of these?" asked Mr. Chips. Mr. Chips put a clean white folded table napkin on each of Oliver's six arms, and Oliver picked up three plates on each arm—one in his hand and two balanced like a real waiter all the way up his arm. And if you can do arithmetic, you will know that means he carried *six* times *three* lots of plates all at once! *Eighteen plates!* Oliver was the best waiter Mr. Chips had ever seen in his life. And eighteen people were all served at once. It didn't take Oliver long to finish that job.

The Tea Clipper

Blow, wind, blow,
Over the tropical sea,
Blow the fine old sailing boat,
Home to you and me,
All the way from India,
Loaded up with TEA.

So, when all the hungry people were happy and eating their lunch, Oliver had another idea. He stood outside the cafe and started juggling with six plates at the same time. He was so clever that he never dropped a single plate. And the people were so pleased that they clapped their hands and threw coins at his feet.

Oliver enjoyed his adventure, but he knew that if he wanted to go back to his family that night, he would have to hurry before the last tide went out. So he collected the coins and put them into a box for poor children who could not have a holiday at the seaside. Then he waved good-by to everyone and went back to the beach. A big wave swooshed on to the beach and swept Oliver back to the bottom of the sea to his brothers. That *was* a lovely adventure, wasn't it?

The Deer Forest

The autumn air was crisp and the sun shone through the pine trees as the group of red deer trotted down the forest path. Melissa, their leader, turned her head to see if her calf was close behind her.

"Hurry up, Sacha," she called. "I smelt danger on the mountainside. We must all go home at once!"

Sacha ran nearer to his mother. "I didn't see anything," he said.

"I heard sounds and saw movements I don't understand. That means danger," replied Melissa.

Sacha said no more. He was very proud of his mother. Every deer in the herd knew that Melissa was their leader.

Deep in the forest Melissa felt safer. As she led the deer towards home she listened to the blackbirds singing; saw rabbits dart away and squirrels playing high in the pine trees. Her sharp eyes even caught a glimpse of a fox slinking by.

"Are we nearly home?" asked Sacha. "I'm tired and hungry."

"We are nearly there, little one," said his mother. "Look! here is the clearing with the woodman's cottage. And there are some bushes near his back door which we like to nibble."

"Well, there is no time to nibble them now, and you must never come here alone. I don't think the woodman means us any harm but it is safer not to go too near humans."

At last they were on their home ground. The hinds, as mother red deer are called, gathered around Melissa. Sacha and his eldest brother trotted off to play.

"Mother says that father will soon be home again," said Sacha.

"Yes," said his brother, "all the stags will be on their way home now from their summer grazing places."

"When we are old enough, will we go with

"I'm sure he's the naughtiest calf in the herd," she grumbled to herself.

Sacha looked up and saw his mother standing in the shelter of the trees.

"Oh, dear," he thought, "I shall get into trouble now, but I was *so* hungry!"

He had trotted halfway towards his mother when a loud roar echoed through the forest, and a large, handsome stag with fine antlers leapt across the clearing.

In her excitement at seeing Sacha's father again, Melissa quite forgot to scold her disobedient son.

I'm Desperate Dan
The cowboy man,
I'm Dangerous Dan Mac Grew,
I ride across the prairie,
When I've nothing else to do.

I chase the badmen
In the west,
In my cart for all to see,
And when I've rescued all my friends,
I go home to tea.

him when he goes away?"

"I expect so. Come on, let's have a race!"

For a moment, Sacha felt sad at the thought of ever leaving his mother, but he soon forgot it in the excitement of the game.

That night, the moon shone so brightly it was almost like day. Melissa stirred, opened her eyes, and looked to see if Sacha was asleep. He was nowhere to be seen.

Filled with alarm, she stood very still, listening for any sound that would tell her that her calf was nearby, but she heard nothing but the wind in the pine trees. Then she remembered something that she had said earlier that day.

Quickly she trotted down the deer path towards the woodman's cottage. The moonlight shone brilliantly as Melissa reached the clearing. She waited for a moment before venturing forward—then she saw Sacha. He was by the woodman's back door, having a fine meal from his favorite bush.

Flowers for the Mayor's Table

The Town Hall clock struck eight as Mrs. Green unlocked her flower shop. The pale sunshine cast shadows on the pavement; the sky was blue; it was going to be a lovely spring day.

She smiled at her Siamese cat, Hi-Lo. He purred loudly and rubbed himself against her legs. Hi-Lo and his mistress went everywhere together.

Mrs. Green looked up at the flags flying from the Town Hall.

"I'm glad it's a fine day," she thought.

At that moment a red van turned into the street and stopped outside the flower shop.

"Here we are, Mrs. Green!" said the driver. "Boxes and boxes of fresh flowers. Where shall I put them?"

"In the workroom, please," answered Mrs. Green and, followed by Hi-Lo, she led the way to the back of the little shop.

The cat sat watching her unpack the boxes and carry the flowers to the bowls of water waiting for them in the shop.

"Look, Hi-Lo," she said, "mimosa and carnations from France!"

Hi-Lo twitched his nose at the sweet smelling blossoms and carefully washed his paws.

Soon the shop was filled with the color of tulips, daffodils, roses, lilac, stately white lilies, small blue gentians, sprays of orchids and simple little bunches of primroses and violets.

Promptly at nine o'clock the shop door opened and a lady came in.

"Good morning, Mrs. Green. I do hope that I'm not too early. How lovely your flowers are!"

"We're quite ready for you," said Mrs. Green. "It's a long time since the Mayor entertained foreign visitors, isn't it?"

"Yes, it is," answered Miss Jones. "There will be important guests from France, Switzerland and Holland, and many other people as well."

"And to think that my flowers will be there to greet them," murmured Mrs. Green to herself.

Miss Jones gave her order briskly and as the last bunch was packed carefully into her car, she turned to Mrs. Green.

"I shall have finished arranging the flowers by eleven o'clock. Would you like to

come and see them before the guests arrive?"

"Oh, yes, I would, very much." said Mrs. Green. "You won't mind if Hi-Lo comes, will you? He walks very well on his leash."

Miss Jones laughed. "I shall be delighted to see you both. I'll meet you at the Town Hall at eleven o'clock. Good-by!"

Right on time Hi-Lo and Mrs. Green climbed the steps of the Town Hall.

"There you are," called a friendly voice and Miss Jones came quickly forward. "Come along, and see your flowers—the Luncheon Room is in here," said Miss Jones.

Hi-Lo stalked through the door in front of Mrs. Green. Portraits hung from the walls, silver and glass glittered everywhere, but the flowers were brightest of all. In honor of each guest there were flowers from his homeland. A bowl of mimosa and carnations for the Frenchman; blue gentians for the gentleman from Switzerland; tulips and hyacinths for the Dutchman, and in front of the Mayor was a simple, but perfect bouquet of primroses and violets.

Mrs. Green smiled. "I have never seen my flowers look so beautiful," she said. "Come along, Hi-Lo, home we go."

George to the Rescue

The winter sky was gray and the wind howled as George, the steam engine, raced through the Canadian countryside. With smoke and sparks flying, he was going as fast as he possibly could and feeling *very* pleased with himself. For George had just passed his rival, Dennis the diesel engine.

Every day, somewhere along the track to Three Rivers Station the two trains met and each tried to race the other home. To George's disgust, Dennis nearly always won.

"He thinks he's going to beat me again, today," chortled George. "Well, I'M going to get there first this time."

"Looks as though we are in for a blizzard," said the fireman, as he shovelled coal into the steam engine's furnace.

"Yes, I shan't be sorry to get home!" shouted the driver.

At that moment, there was a shrill whistle and Dennis rushed past George.

George groaned. "Oh, dear, he's done it again—I shall *never* win," he moaned.

"Nippy trains, those diesels," said George's driver. "But I would much rather

have George—he has never let us down!"

George felt much better.

The next day, it was snowing hard as George's driver and fireman drove him out of his shed into the yard.

"We have been taken off our usual run today," said the fireman, and blew on his hands to keep them warm. "We are going up to the mountains. There is a village up there which has been cut off for days by the snow. We are going to take food and supplies to them. *If* we can get through." he added.

"*I'll* get through," said George to himself, "I may not be all that fast, but I *am* strong."

As he was coupled to two trucks full of provisions, George glanced across at Dennis, who was waiting for his driver.

"Race you home again tonight, George?" asked the diesel jauntily.

"I have more important things to do to-day," said George, "we are going to the rescue of a village!" And before Dennis could utter another word, George gave a loud whistle and steamed out of the yard.

The snow was falling heavily but George pushed it in front of him and the cheery glow from his fire brightened the dark morning.

"We shall soon branch off on to the single track up the valley to the mountains," said the driver, "then we shall not be far from Gorge Tunnel."

Through the valley, with a snow-covered forest on one side and a frozen lake on the other, puffed George. "I wish I came up to the mountains every day," he thought.

As though he knew what George was thinking, the fireman said: "There's nothing to beat an engine like George when it comes to mountain work."

"There's the tunnel ahead!" shouted the driver. "The village is just on the other side."

George's whistle echoed through the valley as he roared in. The tunnel was very dark and very long but then a patch of light appeared and came nearer and nearer. Out of the mountain came George, the trucks rattling behind him—and there, by the side of the track, was a crowd of people, waving and shouting.

George slowed down and stopped.

"We heard you coming up the valley!" shouted someone.

"HOORAY!" yelled the villagers.

In the whole of Canada, there was not a happier or prouder engine than George.

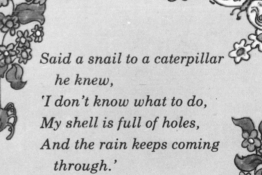

Said a snail to a caterpillar
   he knew,
'I don't know what to do,
My shell is full of holes,
And the rain keeps coming
   through.'

Said the caterpillar
   to the snail with a sigh,
'I'm the one that ought to cry,
I've got so many feet,
I have hundreds of shoes
   to buy.'

Clarabelle
the 'Potty Muss'

Clarabelle is really a baby hippopotamus but as she can't say that word very well, she calls herself a 'Potty muss' which is easier to say. She lives at the zoo in the Hippo park which is like a great big garden without any flowers but with a great big muddy pool in the middle.

The pool is very important because all Hippo's love to have a mud bath and they need lots of room to splash and roll about. Would you like to roll about and splash in the mud? I don't expect so, but Clarabelle loves to do that.

One day, Clarabelle was feeling very excited because it was spring and the sun was shining and at last, after the long cold winter days when very few people came to see the animals, all the children were beginning to visit again.

On this special day, Clarabelle was waiting for someone to come and watch her doing the special trick she had been learning for ages. To pick up a cabbage with her teeth, throw it into the air and catch it in her mouth.

Well, she waited and waited and waited and still nobody came her way. Then she saw two men with a ladder and some buckets on a little cart and they were coming towards the Hippo park. When they got there, she saw that they had a big sign, but of course as she can't read, she didn't know what it said which was *'Please do not feed the Hippos'*.

Anyway, the men came inside the fence, set up the ladder and fixed the sign, they did a bit of painting and then they went away again.

Clarabelle was very interested in all this. She walked slowly over the grass towards the fence and what do you think she found? The buckets of paint had been left behind!

Well, Clarabelle had plenty of fun with them. First she put one foot in the green paint and she looked at it—"Pretty"—she said and in went another foot and another and another until all four feet were bright green. She did laugh, she laughed so much that she knocked the bucket of paint right over and then she slipped on it and soon had flowers to Clarabelle and she was just going to eat them when the wind scattered them in the air and they landed on her back and stuck to the paint. She did look very odd.

I suppose it was all the laughing children that made Clarabelle's Mother come over from the other side of the Hippo park, to find out what was going on, and you should have seen her face when she saw Clarabelle.

"You naughty girl" she said, "what have

a green stripe all down her back from her nose to her tail. She did look funny.

All the green paint was gone then but there was still the blue paint left, so she had a little roll in that as well and made herself into a striped Hippo.

Just as she finished with the paint, she heard the sound of laughing and looking up she saw—what do you think? a row of children all along the fence and all of them were laughing at her.

"How lovely", she thought and she did her little trick with the cabbage and all the children clapped their hands and laughed again. One little boy held out a bunch of

you done to yourself? Hippo's are not supposed to be painted. How are we going to get it off I should like to know?"

But she wasn't really cross, she was trying hard not to laugh as well. She gave Clarabelle a big push with her nose and off they both went to the muddy pool. She washed her and washed her and rolled her in the mud, but still the paint stayed on. Nothing would get it off.

Every day for a week the mother Hippo washed Clarabelle, but the paint would not come off. Secretly, Clarabelle was pleased, because every day the children rushed to see her and she made them laugh and of course she is the only blue and green striped Hippo in the world.

I suppose the paint will wear off some day, but be sure and look out for Clarabelle when you go to the zoo. You might be just in time to see her before it does and she becomes an ordinary plain gray Hippo like the others.

The Present

Jonathan woke up early. "My birthday at last!" he said and he crept to the bottom of his bed and looked over the end. There were his presents arranged on his toy box. That was, all his presents except the one from his mother and father. He knew *that* would not be there, for every year Mother gave it to him herself with a big hug and a "Happy birthday, Jonathan dear!" and that made it very special.

Jonathan picked up a package. It was wrapped in red paper and inside there was a big, bright, double-decker bus. "*With love from Granny and Grandad,*" said the card tucked inside. Jonathan wound up the bus and put his new toy on to the floor.

Away went the new bus with Jonathan dancing behind it. Out of his bedroom and across the passage and, BUMP—the bus ran into the door opposite and stopped. Jonathan was bending down to turn it around when the door opened and his father looked out.

"Hello, young man, so you're up! Many happy returns of the day! My, that's a fine bus!"

"Jonathan!" called his mother. "Bring your other presents into our room and open them here." As Jonathan raced to pick up his packages he wondered excitedly about his present from his mother and father. How he hoped they had not forgotten what he most specially wanted.

He began to think of that day two weeks ago when he had passed the shop with his mother. There it was in the window!

"Oh, look!" Jonathan had cried, pressing his nose against the shop window, "Oh, Mother, I do so wish it could be mine!"

His mother smiled. "Oh, do you, dear? Well, I shall have to speak to Daddy about *that* but if you are a good boy until your birthday perhaps we may have enough pennies to buy it for you, but I can't promise."

Jonathan jumped up and down. "I will be good, Mother, I will really!" he cried.

On the day before his birthday he had passed the shop again and saw that IT was not in the window. Jonathan did not know whether to be glad or sorry. Suppose someone else's mother had bought it? Suppose *his* mother had not been able to find enough

There was a little squirrel
Who lived in the park,
Who had a furry tail
Like a question mark.

money to buy it? Suppose he had not been good enough!

And now as he carried his presents back to his parents' room, his heart thumped with excitement.

"Happy birthday, Jonathan dear," said his mother with a hug. "Here is Daddy with your present from us."

The boy hardly dared to look as his father placed a large, cardboard box carefully on the floor. Then Jonathan heard a tiny whimper and over the side of the box came two small golden paws.

"Oh, you've bought him! You've bought him!" yelled Johathan, "Oh, *thank* you!"

He knelt down and gently lifted from the box a tiny golden Labrador puppy.

"Isn't he the most wonderful dog in the world?" cried Jonathan, joyfully receiving several wet licks.

At breakfast time, after the puppy had had some warm milk, he curled up on a rug in his box and went to sleep.

"We must think of just the right name for him," said Jonathan.

"Yes, we must. Pass the butter, please," replied his father.

"THAT'S what we'll call him," cried Jonathan. "He's just the color of butter. It's a wonderful name. Oh this really is the nicest birthday I've ever had!"

Teddy Koala Bear's secret

Teddy Koala Bear lived in England with Betty. He wasn't English. He was an Australian bear.

Betty thought he was just her toy bear. She didn't know that when she went to sleep at night, he woke up and became a real koala bear. Or that he sometimes went back home to visit his friends in Australia.

But that's what he did.

You see, he'd found an easy and quick way to get there.

He'd found a secret tunnel which went straight through the center of the earth from England to Australia, on the other side of the world. And while other people were busy travelling all round the world by boat or plane to get to Australia, Teddy Koala Bear simply climbed into Betty's toy car and whizzed through the secret tunnel.

He was always back before Betty woke up the next morning.

It was rather lucky that the entrance to the tunnel should be in Betty's garden. Teddy Koala Bear found it exciting whizzing along through the tunnel with the car lights flashing on the walls as he drove along. He always wore a saucepan on his head. He called this his 'crash helmet,' because it made him feel like a real racing driver.

One morning when he came out of the tunnel in Australia—it was morning there, of course—he met his old friend Kandy Kangaroo.

She told him her tummy felt empty.

"Haven't you had any breakfast?" he asked her. "Oh, it's not that," she sighed. "It's because I'm used to my Joey sitting in my pouch, but now he's grown a big boy and doesn't want to ride in it any more, and I feel strange without him."

"Well, you can give me a ride in your pouch," said Teddy Koala Bear.

But, oh dear, he was glad to get out of it

again! When Kandy sprang up in the air and down again it made him feel dizzy. He was glad when she said, "Here's Platypus."

Teddy Koala Bear climbed out quickly. "Hello Platypus," he cried. "Have you decided what sort of an animal you are yet?"

"No," sighed Platypus. "I feel as mixed up as I ever did. Sometimes I feel like a duck. That's when I lay my eggs. Besides, I have a sort of duck's bill. Then other times I feel like a mole. That's when I start burrowing. And then again, I often wonder if I could be a beaver because I'm told my tail is like a beaver's, though I must say I've never seen a beaver."

"Poor Platypus," said Teddy Koala Bear.

"It's not funny to be such a mixed-up sort of animal as you."

But the Kookaburra bird up in the blue-gum tree thought it was funny. Anyway, he started to laugh. And when a Kookaburra bird starts to laugh he never seems to stop until he has everyone else laughing too.

Even Platypus was laughing in the end.

"Stop it, Kooky," cried Teddy Koala Bear. But he was still laughing when they all came to wave Teddy Koala Bear 'good-by' in the tunnel. And *he* laughed all the way back to England.

He must have fallen asleep laughing because when Betty woke up and saw him she said, "Look at Teddy Koala Bear. I believe he's laughing in his sleep."

Cheeky learns a lesson

Tammy had a little puppy called Cheeky. And Tammy knew that when you have a puppy, you must train him to behave properly, especially on the roads.

Tammy had learnt his road rules well a long time ago, and now it was Cheeky's turn to learn and Tammy had to teach him.

So, first he taught Cheeky how to walk properly on the leash, then he showed Cheeky that you only cross the road at the pedestrian crossing. Cheeky was quick to learn this. He also had to wait and look both ways before crossing. Cheeky was very good about that. He sat and looked up at his master and waited until Tammy told him that it was quite safe to cross the road.

Cheeky had to learn. It was a lesson which lots of people forget to teach little boys as well as little puppies. But Tammy knew.

It was that you should only get out of a car on the pavement side. Cheeky took such a long time to learn this. But Tammy never, never let Cheeky off the leash when he was in the car, so Cheeky was quite safe with Tammy.

But there was one lesson Tammy did not teach Cheeky and that was because no one had ever taught Tammy.

One day Tammy and Cheeky were walking along the pavement when Peter-from-across-the-road called out.

"Hi, Tammy!" shouted Peter-from-across-the-road. "How's your puppy?"

Then he started to call the puppy. "Cheeky, come on, Cheeky!"

Cheeky jerked the leash out of Tammy's hand and pounded across the road. Just at that moment a policeman on a bicycle was coming down the road. He missed Cheeky, but one wheel ran over the leash which was trailing behind the puppy. The policeman wobbled off his bicycle.

He put out his big arm and just stopped

Tammy from running right across the road in front of the bicycle too.

"My, my, you haven't learnt your road rules, young man," said the policeman. "That was a silly thing to do!"

"I was trying to save my puppy from being run over," said Tammy.

"But why was your puppy running across the road?" asked the policeman.

"Because I called him," said Peter-across-the-road.

"Ah," said the policeman. "So it was your fault, was it? You must never, never, never call a dog or a little child from across the road. Don't you see how silly it is?"

"Yes," said Peter-from-across-the-road.

"I never thought how dangerous it was either," said Tammy.

"Well you were lucky. None of us was hurt," said the policeman. "There's a Road Safety Exhibition at the Police Station especially for youngsters like you. Ask your mother if you may go. You'll see a lot of interesting things."

Tammy and Peter-from-across-the-road and Cheeky went to the Police Station.

They saw all sorts of pictures of road signs and posters about road safety. The policeman gave them each a big poster to take home and pin on the wall.

And Cheeky had a special little picture of a puppy learning road rules which Tammy pinned up near his basket.

Uncle Harry always late,
Often has to run;
The only way he'll catch his train
Is shot out of a gun!

Uncle Harry has a dream
Of flying through the sky.
But when he comes to earth again
He sees his train flash by.

The Big Juicy Bone

Peter Pup wanted a bone but he didn't know where to find one.

"Where can I get a bone?" he asked the old dog next door.

"From a Butcher's shop of course," said the old dog.

So off went Peter Pup. The first shop had big writing on the door which said DRUGSTORE, but Peter couldn't read. So in he went. There was a smell of bathroom cupboards in the shop—not at all like the smell of delicious bones. "Out you go—no dogs in here," shouted the druggist.

Poor Peter Pup ran out of the shop with his tail between his legs. He must have made a mistake.

The next shop had the words FRUITS AND VEGETABLES on the door. But Peter Pup couldn't read, could he? He went in but this shop smelt like fields and earth—not at all like the smell of big juicy bones. The Storekeeper chased Peter Pup with a broom. "Out —no dogs in here!" he shouted.

The next shop had the word FISH on the door. But Peter Pup couldn't read, could he? So in he went. But this shop smelt like the seaside and summer holidays —all salty—not at all like the smell of nice big juicy bones.

"Out—no dogs in here," said the Fishmonger, pointing a big fat finger at the door.

Peter Pup tried again. The next shop had the word FABRICS on the door. But Peter Pup couldn't read, could he? In he went, but this shop smelt like the linen cupboard at home, where he sometimes crept for a quiet sleep because it was nice and warm in the linen cupboard. Not at all like the smell of nice big juicy bones.

"Is this your dog?" asked the owner. "No," said the lady he was serving.

"Out you go, puppy," said the owner and closed the door behind Peter Pup.

So Peter Pup tried again. The next shop had the word BAKERY on the door. But Peter Pup couldn't read, could he? So in he went.

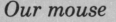

Our mouse

We have a mouse who plays for hours,
In and out of Mother's flowers.
He startles everyone who sees
Him sniffing primroses instead of cheese!

This shop smelt warm and cozy, and crispy and sweet. But it didn't smell at all like big juicy bones. And the Baker clapped his hands and went *"Tut Tut,* we can't have dogs in here!"

Poor Peter Pup! He tried one more shop. This one had the word BUTCHER in big letters on the door. But Peter Pup couldn't read, could he? So in he went.

This shop had Oh! The most delicious smell of sawdust and . . . Peter lifted up his nose and smelt and smelt . . . the most delicious smell of sawdust and . . . *bones!*

"My," he said to himself, because he couldn't talk like ordinary people, could he? "This must be the place!" he said to himself. "I mustn't be chased out of *this* shop!"

So he sat close beside a lady who was buying some meat, and he looked up at her with a loving look, just as if he belonged to her. But the loving look was really for bones, wasn't it?

"Six chops," said the Butcher, "and a bone for your dog," he said kindly. He leant over the counter and gave Peter Pup the biggest, the juicest bone he had ever seen.

Peter Pup ran out of the shop. He wasn't chased out this time, was he? And as he was running out, he heard the lady say: "That's not my dog!"

Peter Pup ran home, and as he passed the old dog next door, the old dog lifted his nose and smelt.

"Where did you get that bone?" he asked grumpily.

"At the Butcher's shop, as you said." said Peter Pup.

That was the biggest juiciest bone Peter pup had ever, ever had. And can you guess where he took it to eat all by himself? In the linen cupboard! He was a naughty pup, wasn't he?

An Important Day

Colin Brown could hardly eat his breakfast, he was so excited. He had some VERY IMPORTANT BUSINESS to attend to with his father, this very morning.

"Hurry up, Colin," said Mr. Brown, "we've got to get started!"

Somehow Colin managed to finish his food.

"That's right," said mother, "now come and put your coat on while Daddy is getting out the car."

"Ready, Colin?" called father.

"Coming, Dad!" shouted the boy. "Good-by, Mother!"

Colin always enjoyed the drive to the nearby town and soon they were turning into the parking field behind High Street.

Eagerly, Colin looked around him as they walked up High Street—then he saw it.

"There it is, Daddy! It's red and white and it's turning round and round!"

"That's right," said father, "whenever you see a striped pole like that one, you will find a barbershop. I think I will have my hair cut, too."

As Mr. Brown opened the shop door it gave a loud *Ping,* and as he followed his father inside, Colin saw four large black, leather chairs in a row. They were facing four large mirrors. In each of the chairs someone was having his hair cut. Along one wall stood a line of empty wooden chairs.

"Well, that's lucky," said father, "we are next. Come and sit down here, Colin, until it's our turn."

Colin sat watching the scissors snipping and cutting and listening to the friendly chatter all around him.

"I like it in here, Dad," he said. "Will I have to sit in one of those chairs? They look awfully big!"

Mr. Brown smiled. "Yes, you will," he said. "Ah it's our turn, now!"

Two empty chairs waited for them.

"My son would like his hair cut," said Mr. Brown "and I'll have mine done as well, please."

"Certainly, sir," said the barber, "if you will sit here, my Mr. Smith will cut yours, and I shall attend to this young man."

He took a large, black leather cushion and put it in Colin's chair.

Colin climbed into the seat and smiled shyly into the mirror.

"Ever had your hair cut in a shop before?" enquired the barber, whisking a white cape round the boy's shoulders.

"No, I haven't," said Colin, growing pink.

"Then this *is* an important day, isn't it? Now I'm just going to tuck a band of soft paper around your neck inside your sweater, so that the hairs won't tickle you!"

The barber quickly combed Colin's hair, then picked up his scissors—he was ready to start.

"Now, bend your head and don't wriggle if you can possibly help it!" he said.

Snip, snip went the scissors. Colin kept very still.

"Raise you head, please. That's fine!"

Colin watched as his hair was trimmed and shaped, just like his father's.

Now the barber was busy brushing the loose hairs away from the boy's neck.

"Shut your eyes," he commanded. "I'm going to squirt your hair with something to keep it tidy."

When Colin opened his eyes, again, Mr. Brown was smiling down at him. "Well done, Colin," he said, "you behaved like a real man, I'm proud of you!"

The Balloonist

Grandfather who lived in days gone by,
Said to Grandma, 'Why don't we fly?
Let's take a balloon up ever so high,
Up into the bright blue sky.'

'We'll eat our lunch and have our tea,
As we glide over the deep blue sea,
We'll be safe in the basket and have
   such fun,
As we drift into the setting sun.'

Harry the Helicopter

The big planes at the airport were talking excitedly, "buzz, buzz, buzz." They were so busy talking they didn't notice Harry Helicopter arrive.

"Hello, everyone," called Harry.

The big planes stopped talking then, and looked at him. "Oh," cried one. "It's only little grasshopper."

That was their nickname for Harry Helicopter. They said he hopped about like a grasshopper. They made fun of him really.

Harry didn't care. "They may fly to far away places," he told himself. "But I can do something none of them can do. I can rise straight up into the air and come down where I like without having to use a 'runway'."

It always amused him to see the big planes circling round in the sky waiting their turn to land.

And the fuss they made about it all when they did land. Even when they touched ground they taxied along the runway, first this way, then that way before they at last came to a halt. Even then they stopped sometimes far away from the airport building and the passengers had to board a bus to get there. Just imagine it.

Harry Helicopter gave a little chuckle at the thought.

Now he could land on a flat roof of a house—and had often done so. Oh yes, there was no cause to make fun of him.

But what was this the big planes were saying now? A strange plane was coming to land at the airport?

"There's fog at the airport where it usually lands and it's been told to come here instead," said one of the big planes.

"It's bringing an important person, and he will be upset when he lands here, because this is too far away from where he needs to be," said another plane.

"Here comes the plane now," cried another big plane.

They all watched as the strange plane circled round and round above the airport. Then down it came and at last the 'important person' stepped out.

But there was no fuss and bother as the big planes had expected. Oh no. The important person simply walked across and stepped

into the waiting Harry Helicopter.

And in next to no time Harry flew off and landed him exactly where he needed to be.

He was delighted and said so to Harry's pilot. He even gave Harry a pat as he hurried off.

The next time Harry went to the airport the big planes stopped talking as soon as they saw him. They didn't call him grass-hopper either, they called him Harry.

They were eager to know if he'd taken any more important persons anywhere.

"I'm doing it all the time," said Harry. "Sometimes I take sick people to hospital. And sometimes I go to rescue people from boats that have struck a rock, or drifted out to sea. I may not fly to far away places like you, but I don't wish to. I'd rather be helping people who are in trouble—or wanting to get somewhere quickly."

The big planes didn't know what to say. They'd no idea that Harry led such an interesting life. They never made fun of him again.

Not that Harry cared. He was much too busy to bother.

A Goat in the Garden

William, the goat, was a fine fellow. He had handsome horns, a long beard and bright, mischievous eyes.

Most of the time he was content to live in the meadow belonging to Plum Tree Cottage. He had a comfortable hut to shelter in, and he was quite used to being tethered to the beech tree by a rope fastened to his leather collar. In fact, the rope was so long that often he forgot he was tied up at all.

But sometimes, when he heard the children playing in the cottage garden, he longed to join in. On one sunny afternoon, the meadow was bright with buttercups; swallows were darting about the sky and exciting noises were coming from the garden.

"I am going to see what is happening," thought William. He set off towards the meadow gate. Suddenly, he stopped with a jerk. He had come to the end of his rope.

"Now, what shall I do?" he grunted, "I know, I'll just pull, and pull, and pull!" And that naughty goat tugged and he pulled until, SNAP! the rope parted!

William snorted joyfully and trotted through the gate into the garden.

The children, Robin and Jenny, were sitting on a rug sipping lemonade and eating cream buns. Mother was handing a cup of tea to Aunt Martha who was leaning comfortably back in her deck chair. Aunt Martha loved hats, especially summer ones, and a very smart straw hat lay on the grass by her side.

Now, Aunt Marther was not the only one to like straw hats, William loved them, too; they tasted so delicious! His eyes sparkled and he moved quietly forward towards Aunt Martha's chair. Just then mother saw him.

"WILLIAM!" she cried, "what *are* you doing here? Go back to the meadow!"

William lowered his head. "Shan't!" he thought excitedly and, missing the hat with his mouth, he stuck one of his horns through it and charged off.

"My hat! My hat!" wailed Aunt Martha. "Someone save it, please!"

"Children, bring William's rope. I will try and tempt him back with a cake!" cried mother.

Shaking with laughter, Jenny and Robin ran off to do as they were bid. But William did not mean to be caught so soon, he was

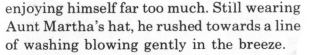

enjoying himself far too much. Still wearing Aunt Martha's hat, he rushed towards a line of washing blowing gently in the breeze.

Blackie, the cat, who had been asleep in the washing basket, sat up. He arched his back and his fur bristled.

"Hello, cat!" snorted William.

Blackie spat loudly, and ran up the clothes line pole.

"How rude!" thought William, "I shall chase him!"

Once more, he lowered his head and charged. Down came mother's washing and away flew Blackie to the orchard. Scattering clothes all around him, William gave chase.

"My washing!" cried mother.

From the branches of an apple tree, Blackie glared down at William as the goat pushed against the tree. But William had forgotten one thing. A family of geese lived in the orchard.

"Look at that stupid goat in a hat!" said the gander. "We don't want him here, let's give him a fright!"

With necks outstretched, hissing loudly and looking *very* fierce, they rushed at William.

The goat stood still. "Oh," he thought, "I don't like geese, I'm off!"

"Caught you!" cried Robin and slipped the rope through William's collar.

Aunt Martha came and rescued her battered hat. William looked at her and wondered whether he might still try to nibble it.

"Perhaps not," he decided, "those geese have spoilt all my fun."

And William meekly allowed himself to be led back to his beech tree.

Stories written by the four authors
appear on the following pages